Living Portals: A Collection of Sci-Fi Stories

Tim L. Thompson

Acknowledgments:

Many thanks to my wife and both my kids for encouraging me to push through and get these stories out there. Thanks to Nicholas McMillan for editing my drafts and providing thoughtful comments and hard work to get the drafts ready for publication. Thanks to all the many contacts I have who've visited my blog, commented on my social media postings and otherwise helped to get my work out there.

Table of Contents

Bury the Evidence: A Portal Story I

"We're safe. We can relax now. Let's go look up the right acid to buy..."
Tom Tedesco

We'd been gone for three days. We were back in an instant. Half an arm lay wriggling in a pool of blood on the floor.

"That was way, way too close!!" Helga screamed. We both looked down at the severed arm writhing on the hardwood floor beneath us. Then she continued, "Couldn't you keep him from chasing us in and losing his arm?"

"I know how to get us through a portal, not how to stop someone who's chasing us!" I squawked out as my voice cracked.

Helga started blurting out random phrases, "I can't look at that . . . did we make it . . . are we safe?" She was dancing pitter pat in little circles on the den floor as she randomly shrieked out each word and phrase.

"Yes, we made it. We are safe now." As blood started oozing out of the loose limb on the floor, I tried to flatten my voice to put on a false bravado, "I'll clean it up." I wasn't sure if I was trying to be more reassuring for Helga or for myself as I went to the kitchen to get a black plastic garbage bag, but, *"Where will I bury that thing?"* and, *"How can I destroy it?"* kept rolling through my head.

Helga had stepped out of the den, where we had reentered our home from the portal. As I passed her, I noticed the nice frame she still carried even at 48. Cycling class wasn't wasted on her. "I'm going to put that arm in the garage, and I can clean up the blood with hydrogen peroxide," I told her. "But then what . . ." My voice trailed off.

I walked back into the den, where the cat was still peacefully sleeping on her favorite armchair, not having stirred from our reappearance at all.

"You'd think after seven days we might get a welcome purr or a rub?" I mused.

Then I awkwardly scooped a still-twitching, severed arm into the thick, black plastic garbage bag from the kitchen.

"They can't figure out how to follow us can they?" Helga's voice trembled as she queried me from the hallway, her striking blue eyes widening more than I ever remembered.

"We figured out how to manipulate a portal and get there, so who knows! Maybe someday they'll figure out how to get here." I was just taking notice of a calendar clock anomaly when I heard someone at the door.

Thud, thud . . . We were interrupted by a loud knocking. I walked over casually to see who it was.

My color drained as I looked out of the peephole . . . police!

Helga came up behind me. "Who is it?" she said.

"It's the police," I managed to softly squeak out. The color drained out of her face too.

"This is just an odd coincidence," I tried to say reassuringly. But I knew full well that events in dimensions often paralleled each other. This, I'd been told in a past foray, happened more frequently between dimensions where mutual crossings occur. "I'm going to need to explore that characteristic of portals more in the future," I notched in my memory just as I was snapped back to reality by the policemen banging on the door again.

Whack, whack . . . went the door as I stood in front of it, suddenly very keenly aware of the severed arm I was carrying in my black plastic kitchen bag. My mind was racing, "I just committed mayhem on a policeman from another dimension . . . unwittingly, but still, it happened." I told my mind, "Be still. There's no way the police from the other dimension would even know we were from another dimension, let alone know how to call our police and get them here so quickly." I dropped the dead arm bag to the side of the door, away from the door's opening, and I cracked open the door, leaving the chain lock in place, all while trying to keep Helga and her terrified looks out of the general view.

"Hi officer, what's up?" I said with a falsely chipper voice.

"Hi, are you Tom Tedesco?" the officer queried.

"Yes," I replied.

"We've had a complaint about loud crackling noises, humming sounds, and possible shots fired in the neighborhood. Have you seen or heard anything unusual?" the officer jumped right into his investigation.

I froze for several seconds thinking about all the unusual things I'd seen and heard for the last three days: people who could regrow limbs, people with tails, and people who were literally cold-blooded like reptiles.

"No, I can't say I have." I tried to say in a calm voice, but the officer didn't seem to accept my attempt at calm reassurance.

"Are you sure?" he quizzed again. "Apparently the noises were quite loud, and several neighbors thought the sounds came from here."

"This house?" I said as I started to feel a little braver. "No, nothing here. But we're well insulated, so we wouldn't hear it if a car crashed in our driveway." That was a lie, but it sounded pretty good coming out. Or, that's what I thought. Besides, I thought to myself, "What shots did they hear? We were on the other side of the portal when that policeman shot at us . . . and that was just moments ago."

"Would you mind if we came in?"

Now the officer was getting a bit too pushy and pesky for my liking.

"Yes, I'd mind," I said. "We are on vacation and cleaning up the house, and my wife isn't fully dressed at the moment." A convenient lie, but I was grasping for responses.

The officer's face turned six shades of red and purple. I'm pretty sure I saw lilac, salmon, and even fuchsia in his cheeks. "I need to see what's going on," he said as he started to lean forward to peer in.

"There's no evidence of imminent danger here, and I'm tired. If you want to search my house, get a warrant." I slammed the door and bolt locked it. Sweat started pouring all over my body. I kept my right eye glued to the peephole. The two officers started arguing the merits of breaking my door down versus getting a warrant. Thankfully, it appeared the warrant argument won out as they painstakingly inched back to their car parked along the curb. I sighed heavily as they pulled away, but I was now soaked in sweat.

"We've got to get rid of that thing ASAP!" I snapped out. Helga was soaking wet with sweat too and looked like she might faint when my sudden outburst snapped her back to the present.

"Let's get it in the 4Runner!" she raggedly exclaimed.

We ran to the garage, threw the bag with the severed arm in the truck, and then another thought came to me.

I practically shouted, "We need to bury the arm in the woods at the edge of the neighborhood until we can get some acid to melt it into nothing".

"What?" she croaked out.

"Seriously," I said, "we need to completely annihilate it so that no one can trace it, find it, follow it, link it to us . . . you get me."

Helga looked lost for a minute, but the fact was we couldn't leave the arm here in case the police came back quickly as we weren't yet prepared to destroy it. We didn't regularly keep high powered acid on the shelf in the garage. So she slowly accepted it as the best short run alternative to just waiting to see if the police would come back with a warrant.

We waited long enough for the first round of questioning cops to be cleared out of the neighborhood. I had Helga walk from our house to the last house at the end of the cul-de-sac, which sits just in front of the edge of the woods. "Lucky we live on the edge of town," hummed in my mind. She scanned back to our house and waved to indicate all was clear.

I raced out with severed arm bag in hand. We jogged over to the backyard of the house that sits in front of the woods. Then we ran down a trail behind the house and climbed into a ravine that ran down towards the river. When we got deep enough, I took us off the trail and into some briars. I had thought to grab a small shovel from the neighbor's back yard as we went through it to get to the trail. It only took about an hour and a half, but we dug about two and a half feet down and buried the arm. Relief for now . . . time to go find acid . . . strong acid.

When we got back to the top of the trail and into the back of our neighbor's yard, we both let out a sigh of relief, and Helga cried a little to let some of her tension out.

"Let's get back to the house," I panted, a little too exhausted from our prior adventure and the climb down the trail.

But as we started back into the cul-de-sac, a neighbor from one of the houses between ours and the last house before the trail, Ben Mosely, was coming towards us. Ben was a squirrely guy who bothered me even though he'd never done anything wrong to me. He was just annoying and buggy with his awkward toupee, his weird eye twitches and smiles that seemed like they were bent into and out of place.

"What have you two been up to?" he prodded us with a serious look just before he cracked a wide grin. At first I thought he was just being friendly, but there was a small shiftiness in his left eye just after he smiled. I tried a fake laugh to allay any concerns he had about our activities in the woods.

"Ha, we were having a lover's get away down in the old woods . . ." It sounded worse when it came out.

"Actually, ah, we just needed the exercise," I tried again. That one seemed to work.

"Can't get enough of that," Ben cackled while patting his belly. Still, I think he noticed that Helga was stiff and looked like she was about to break down (despite her rather awkward fake smile and laugh).

Then Ben surprised us with this little gem, "you know, when I saw you two out planting flowers this morning, I thought to myself, that nice couple seem like the type to have secret adventures. I bet you two are always up to something that the rest of us wish we could be up to."

We hurried back to the house, but I kept glancing back at Ben. We've been gone for three days, what was he talking about seeing us planting flowers this morning.

At the front porch Helga couldn't contain it any longer, "Tom, we've been gone three days, but Ben thinks he saw us planting flowers this morning. We planted flowers three days ago before we left. Is he suffering from some type of dementia?"

"No Helga, I saw the calendar clock in the house earlier and I thought there had been a power outage, but now I think that the three days we were gone was only about two or three hours back here. Apparently portals cross time as well as space." Helga looked like she might pass out from that little revelation again, but I pointed back at Ben to distract her. We watched as he continued to wander around near the other neighbor's backyard.

He looked towards the back edges of the neighbor's lawn as it led to the trail but made no effort to go down it. He held his arms up like he was praying . . . or trying to sense something—that worried me. But he didn't seem like he felt whatever he was hoping for. After we got in our house, I watched back out the window. Ben didn't proceed into the trail area, but he was painstakingly slow at walking back to his own house.

"Can this be over?" wailed Helga. "I can't take this stress! We were somewhere we don't belong, we have seriously injured a man from some other time or place, and now the police want a warrant for our house!" She was shot. I hugged her and said, "We're safe. We can relax now. Let's go look up the right acid to buy."

The last two sentences weren't really congruent. But, Helga relaxed, and we felt . . . safe.

"We're in the clear now," I told myself.

The sky was blue outside as I looked out our front window into the cul-de-sac and out over towards the woods. All looked calm.

. . . Somewhere down in the ravine, the dirt over a tiny, fresh grave started shifting.

Wolf's Blood: A Portal Story II

*He had wolves to his left and bloodthirsty men to his right. He
pushed through the snow, to the northeast, but he was fighting a
losing battle... "I wonder if I could introduce my predators
to each other..."*

The sound of snow and ice cracking under his boots and snow-
shoes grew tiresome as he powered forward. Ice was crunching all
around him as he lumbered ahead into the storm. Snap! Brittle tree
limbs were falling all around, from the weight of too much snow.
Even what seemed like healthy trees were losing limbs. He was in
near whiteout conditions now, and he was cursing himself for lack
of a guide.

He'd been warned not to go the five miles from the supply outpost to his cabin without a guide along. He was too new to the area.
An older trail hand at the outpost had offered to go the five miles
with him, but he was proud of his outdoor skills and wanted to
stand on his own. Now he could barely stand as he sank into drifts
and kept pushing towards the cabin. He passed the three-quarters
eaten, frozen remains of a rabbit torn apart by some tundra predator that had raced away to pursue a fresher prize (or been chased
away by a bigger predator).

"Ugh . . . gak . . ." he choked back his lunch, "I don't want to end
up like that."

He'd started out from the outpost with a snowmobile, a sack of
supplies, and about four hours of available sunlight. But the snowmobile couldn't cut it past about a mile. The wind and snow made
driving it a risk. He'd nearly run into trees several times as he could

barely see more than four or five feet ahead. So, he abandoned it and plodded ahead on his own.

He'd climbed off the snowmobile and headed northeast towards the cabin in the general area of the now well-blanketed path he was used to following. He had the bag of supplies and a high caliber rifle on his shoulder as he tried to keep his balance and momentum on snow shoes in the twenty below weather. He thought he was at least at the halfway point when he heard wolves in the distance.

"I thought even they would be hunkered down in this mess." He nervously mulled over in his head as to why they would be out in these conditions, "Maybe they're hoping for some easy prey that is struggling." It wouldn't be him. He pushed forward again.

Movement was getting very difficult. Balance, perception, and direction were problematic now. His clothes, while state of the art arctic apparel, were getting too loaded with snow, and any breach or breakdown might allow moisture to get in contact with his skin and cause frost bite. He needed to pause. Then he heard the howls again, "Awoow . . . aroo . . ."

"Crap . . . they're getting closer . . ." He pondered his next actions carefully and decided to stop and light a fire. He needed the break, and the fire would give him some warmth and allow him to check his gear.

He got his compass and navigational gear out to verify his location and progress. A quick summary of things showed he was off course and south of his intended path by a quarter mile and about two and a half miles out from the outpost. So he had traveled half the needed distance, but he still had to cover sixty percent of the route to get there after accounting for the extra half mile he'd have to compensate for. Worse, he was truly in a no man's land area. He knew wolves were nearby, and soon he'd be running out of daylight.

He got a flint striker tool out and found some brush immediately nearby. He spotted a set of trees that provided a backdrop alee of the wind. He lit the fire and got more visibility as the wind paused for a moment. That's when he realized that the fire was a bad, bad idea.

The wolves were hoping for prey that was alone and out loose in the storm. They had been upwind of Tom. But there was a brief pause in the wind, and the light from the fire lit up his area and made him a target . . . And they were much closer than he had perceived. Now they knew he was there, and the howls they were giving off started to border on the macabre. His internal fear indicators lit up. Goosebumps on the arms, hair standing up along the back of his neck, and throat getting constricted, he was in trouble. He knew it, and his body knew it (and didn't mind telling him so). It was time to go.

"Oh crap, oh crap . . ." He was racing for solutions in his head, "I need to light up the flares and drag them around me. No, no time for all that, and I don't know if it would help at all." Other crazy ideas were forming quickly. "I could shoot several," he thought, "but that sounds like a large pack, and, if they close too quickly, I can't get them all. Maybe if I could shoot one quickly, they'd back off . . ." Then the wind picked up, and visibility went back to about four to five feet for Tom. The fire struggled to stay lit.

Tom grabbed up all his gear, stomped out the fire, and started moving again, headed in the direction of the cabin. His body was aching from the work now, and the snow hadn't gotten any easier to get the snow shoes on top of. The wolves were to his left side and still a few hundred yards away. He kept the rifle ready, but he was starting to consider dropping some of the supplies in his bag to lighten the load. He could tell from the occasional howl that the wolves were rapidly closing in, but he could not see them to take any accurate shot as twilight was coming on.

He'd gotten his pace to about as close as possible to a run under the circumstances, but it just expended more energy. It didn't move him that far and increased all sorts of risks. And then it happened . . . an unexpected shift in the terrain. "Oh no . . . gahh," he blurted out nonsense as he was tumbling down a small ravine and losing supplies and his sense of direction. He heard the sound of a rifle shot not too far off in the distance. Then . . . Kathunk! He hit the bottom of the ravine and hadn't broken any bones or lost his rifle. Most importantly, there were no tears in his clothing! "Small miracles," he thought to himself. He didn't value the lost cabin supplies at all at this point, but he did have a small pack of food, fire-starter materials, and navigational tools in a belt bag that had not come loose and that he was thankful to hold onto.

"Where are the wolves . . ." he hissed to himself, ". . . no howling." He'd actually accelerated quite a bit on the tumble and slide and increased the distance from the wolves quite favorably. The wolves had paused as they were trying to relocate his scent and grasp his movement and direction. The slide off the hill and into the ravine had thrown them off, but not for long.

Tom heard them start up again while he was re-determining his location and the proper course towards the cabin. Then he heard the sound of men's voices . . . very close. He stood up on a small mound in the snow and the wind paused once again. He saw two men, a tall man with a tattoo of what looked like a large rat on his neck and a fat man with a too-thick-for-class moustache. They were standing over a third man who was lying on his side in the snow and bleeding from the back of his parka. He looked like he'd been shot. Then one of the two standing men looked up and saw Tom before he could duck.

"Hey, what are you doing there!" called the man.

Tom did not want to wait to discuss why they had shot a man in the back in the middle of a snowstorm. The wind picked up and shut down visibility again. He had wolves to his left and blood-thirsty men to his right. He pushed through the snow, to the northeast, but he was fighting a losing battle. The wolves had closed in during his pause to recalibrate his position, and the men were right on his tail. He felt the only reason they hadn't fired on him yet was the low visibility from the snowstorm and the trees that were providing cover as he stomped ahead.

"I wonder if I could introduce my predators to each other," rolled into his head. Tom chuckled to himself. "That was the best idea I've come up with in a year . . . But how do I facilitate it?"

"I need another ravine to slide down, but boy will that introduce risks," he pondered as the two groups of predators closed the gap on him and unwittingly closed the gap on each other. His heart was pounding and despite the constant cracking and crunching sounds of the ice and snow, the loudest sound he could hear now was the sound of his own breathing efforts. He had to constantly turn into the parka hood or cover his mouth with his mitts to breath due to the extreme cold. He was not going to be able to maintain this. Then a small hill with a backside not unlike the earlier ravine presented itself.

Tom didn't wait to calculate approaches or descent speed. He dove into the ravine in a crazed, awkward slide. As he went into the slide, there was an odd shimmer at the bottom of the hill that caught his eye. No time to consider any risk from it. He caromed off small bumps in the hill and slid ahead. If he hit a rock and broke a bone, he was a goner.

"Is that a light from someone's camp . . . or a mirror someone left in the woods . . ." He could barely make it out in the driving snow. However, as he hoped, the snow and the hill worked together to give Tom a gap between himself and his pursuers. Swish . . . he was at the bottom of the hill just as the men came over the top and were apparently debating the slide down themselves. The wolves had come around the side of the hill and were about the same distance from Tom, maybe sixty to seventy yards away but just to the north, whereas the men were to the southwest. Yet neither group had spotted each other yet. "They're still too focused on me," Tom giggled to himself now despite the churning in his stomach. "This might actually work," he hoped deliriously.

Tom turned around to see where the shimmering light had come from, and then he looked up. There at the base of the hill was a shimmering, seven-foot-tall section of what looked like a liquid mirror. He backed towards it (to keep his eyes on the pursuing groups above him) and threw some snow at it. There was a slight humming noise and the shimmer swallowed it. "Where did that snow go?" he was stunned. Then a howl broke his attention free from the shimmer.

He turned to see that the men and the wolves had arrived almost simultaneously. At this point, they were within thirty yards of him.

"Hello," shouted Tom up at the men, "please meet my friends." He pointed to the wolves. The wolves had briefly paused to assess the arrival of the two men. Tom realized that it was indeed a large pack . . . the largest he'd ever encountered. One by one, they were arriving, and there were about nine as Tom could assess. That's when

Tom realized he wasn't the only one who'd been trying to set the men up. There was another group of two wolves coming up behind and to the left of them.

The alpha wolves, which were out front, weren't waiting too long, and neither were the men. A frenzy of shooting and attacking started when Tom realized there were two wolves behind him . . . But the shimmer was between them.

Wild thoughts spring from desperate moments. "I don't know what that is, but, at this point, it may be my safest option." Tom sprung forward toward the shimmer, hoping maybe it was just a fancy mirrored hide-out for hunters or some kind of militarized camouflaged hole that was being tested by the army in these deep woods. He didn't really care. He just needed a way out of the jam he was in.

He jumped at and fell through the shimmer and out on the other side, discovering it was a portal. A seemingly natural one but a portal to another realm. He was still in deep woods, but there was no snow here at all, and the temperature was mild. Then a wolf burst through too! "Crap . . . shoot it . . ." he started to yell at himself when it fell to the ground yelping a sharp, brief shriek, and he realized only half of the wolf had made it through. The head and half of a bloody torso now lay before him oozing wolf's blood onto the beautiful moss and grass covered forest floor. The front half of the wolf but not the back had made it through. "Well, half a wolf is way better than a whole!" Tom burst out with laughter at himself. Then he threw up his lunch all over the new forest floor.

"Ok, that was too perfect," he said aloud as he wiped the vomit from his mouth and chin. Inwardly, Tom's realization that the now halved wolf torso could have been him was quite discomforting. No more wolves were following, nor were the two men. The shimmer hummed and buzzed a bit and then evaporated in a puff.

"Now, how do I get back . . . and where am I? Tom was quizzing himself as he looked around in a stupor at what looked like pictures he'd seen of a European forest from the Middle Ages. "You know Tom, they have wolves in Europe too," he warned himself. As he inspected his immediate surroundings, he found a sign lying slumped over beside a nearby pathway. On it was written, *Autoroute du roi*.

"Guess I should have taken French," Tom mused, figuring the meaning of the sign was something about a roadway.

On the other side of the now disintegrated shimmer, was a large party of men who'd arrived just in time to save the two men Tom ran from. This was followed by much shooting and wolves running amok before leaving to come another day. At this point, the number of humans had increased enough that the wolves decided to flee en masse.

As he surveyed the carnage and remains around him, the mustachioed fat man asked, "You don't think that was the newcomer that everyone's calling Tom running from us do you Greg?"

The tall man with the tattoo of the rat was curious too, "I think maybe it was, sheriff. I think that he thought we'd shot that guy that we'd just cornered. I can see how that would have looked bad from his perspective." He smiled a shifty, nasty little smile.

"I just wish we could have gotten to him before he disappeared. Where do you think he got off to?" the sheriff continued.

"I don't know, it was like he just vanished. I saw a weird reflection at the base of that hill like a mirror or sheet of metal right before he ducked behind it. Still odd that there was nothing down here when we got here. Maybe a snow mirage? But," he continued, "he's going to need to answer how he cut that wolf in half. How do you suppose he did that and where did the other half of the wolf go?" the deputy asked rhetorically.

"It's been a strange night. I'm just glad the rest of the search party got here when the wolves encircled us," said the sheriff.

"Me too," said Deputy Halverson. He picked up the back half of a bloody wolf carcass and threw it in a sack to take back to forensics for further investigation.

"See you back at the station Greg," said Sheriff Thompson as he climbed into a waiting Snocat.

Meanwhile, Tom was pondering his predicament and the meaning of the fallen sign while sitting on a stump in a beautiful but unknown forest.

Behind and above him a small, slender figure was peering out from her perch upon a tree limb. "Well, it's about time we had fresh blood . . ." she said softly. "He'll do fine, just fine . . ."

All Wet: A Portal Story III

"Portals come in threes . . . if you wait for a third, you can take it back home." – Ben Mosely of N.M.

She was standing over a dead body and trying to revive him with CPR. His boots and outer wear lay strewn about him. Blood from his gunshot wound was still dripping on the ship deck.

"He's not responding," I said firmly.

We'd seen a flash of shimmering light and then saw a man fall, seemingly from the sky, onto the deck of our ship. We'd run the length of our benefactor's yacht and gotten to him right as he collapsed on the deck and started going into shock. Helga, upon getting to him, had immediately slipped off his parka—yes, a parka—and outer clothes. I plugged the bullet wound I saw on his back with a spray-on, artificial skin patch we had in the med kit, and Helga started doing CPR when he went catatonic and unresponsive.

Helga and I were meteorological scientists, and we'd gotten a unique opportunity to do ocean-based, atmospheric research in the Atlantic on a small, private yacht that belonged to a research think tank funded by an eccentric billionaire. I did think it odd that we'd never met him, but he seemed very convinced that Helga and I were the right scientists to take his ship and do research for him. His goals, which were also somewhat unclear as of yet, seemed odd. He just asked us to record weather anomalies and measure all atmospheric conditions at certain precise locations and times. Yet I remember feeling oddly comfortable as he called us and set out the various research he wanted done. He wouldn't introduce himself, and he was only known, even by the staff at the research headquarters, as Mr. Ted (so close to my own name Tom Tedesco that I found it an amusing coincidence).

The yacht had been rigged with all types of meteorological equipment and the ability to load and unload crews and large equipment from the sides of the ship while at sea. Our first crew all got sick from a flu outbreak, and because Helga was an experienced and trained ship captain as well, we'd left without them. The research think tank had agreed, even encouraged us, to proceed without the crew so that we would not fall behind our benefactor's research timelines. So we'd left them back at the dock, with the understanding that a new crew would be flown out in about a week.

"I don't understand where he came from, Tom?" said Helga quizzically before going into a tirade, "We're in the middle of the Atlantic Ocean, a few hundred miles west of Santa Cruz Das Flores, with nothing but sea birds in sight. It's about 86 degrees and sunny, and this freezing cold guy with a parka on and a gunshot wound in his back climbs onto our boat and collapses . . . and other than some ice on his boots and pants, he's dry as a bone. Where's his boat?!?!"

"And why was he wearing a parka, and what was that shimmering light we saw right before he showed up?" I followed up. I pondered if he'd blown his boat up or lit it on fire right before he spotted us and climbed aboard, but there were no explosion sounds and no sign of debris or a boat of any type anywhere to be seen (and I kept looking while Helga was giving him CPR).

Helga had stopped the CPR. His body lie stiff and prone, and then suddenly exploded with "Gackhhggh...flargllgh." The guy seized and coughed up what sounded like half a lung and started to gasp for air. "I didn't do it!" he wheezed out.

"Relax," Helga demanded him to be still, and he acquiesced, but . . .

"I didn't do it," he kept pleading.

"We accept your plea," I said sardonically.

"Tom!" Helga objected to my tone, "He was nearly dead. Give him a minute."

So we did. We sat and waited on him to stabilize . . . which he did. Then Helga went about getting him to agree and started removing the bullet from his backside. That stint she did as an EMT in South America always seemed to come in handy.

"There's not actually that much damage from the bullet. I think it was from a small caliber weapon. I think he was going into shock from the trauma and possibly exposure or hypothermia. Do you think he was stuck in a freezer on his boat?" Helga tried to make sense out of the situation.

I was past that point and wanted to interrogate the guy, but Helga cut me off as I started and said we had to get him to a bed where he could rest.

I didn't want to ruin any bedrooms for our soon to be arriving crew. Luckily, the yacht had a small guest bedroom into which we'd just stuffed miscellaneous supplies and gear when space was needed elsewhere. I went down into the hull, and I threw the mess here and there, grabbing supplies and stuffing them into cabinets that snapped shut to keep things from spilling all over the boat. Then, I cleared a path for our unexpected guest so that Helga and I could drag him down the steps together and get him into the guest room. We put him into the tiny guest bed, covered him, and let him start the recovery process.

We took turns checking on him, bringing him drinks, and feeding him. We were able to get basic information from him such as the facts that his name was Ben Mosely and he was from Picacho, New Mexico, but Helga strictly limited our conversations to keep him restful. Ben actually showed signs of recovery pretty quickly. This supported Helga's theory that the gunshot wound, while not pleasant, was from a small caliber weapon that really hadn't done too much damage. It hadn't been deep when Helga extracted it, and it wasn't terribly destructive to the skin tissue in and around the wound. Lastly, his reactions were more like that of someone being injured in an extreme environment (like the arctic) and going into shock. We all took a restless night of sleep.

The next day, Helga and I went down to the guest bedroom after running our normal morning atmospheric tests on deck. Ben was able to start conversations with us, and we immediately started peppering him with questions like: "How did you get here?" "Why were you wearing a parka?" "How did you get shot?" "Are you still in danger?" and "Where's your boat . . . ????"

"I can tell you all about that," he was trying to reply in the middle of our questions. Along with a lot of "I'll explain" or "Let me get to that," and he finally exclaimed, "Let me start at the beginning!"

"Please do!" I said with exasperation. I couldn't wait for this story to get going.

"I was outside my home in New Mexico. I was taking a walk outside when I spotted a large shiny object shimmering out on the edge of town near my home but outside our neighborhood, in the glade. I thought maybe it was a UFO. I was excited and ran out to investigate." Ben started to get animated now.

"As I approached the object closer, I saw that it looked like a tall mirror, 10 or 11 feet tall and maybe six feet wide. It looked like a liquid mirror that would reflect some of the surroundings nearby, but it distorted them too."

I jumped in, "So you saw a giant, reflective liquid mirror in the glade and ran towards it?" Then, I picked at Ben, "Did aliens jump out?" while I thought to myself, "Why would I say that? I've just seen a shimmering light produce a nearly frozen man in a Parka with a fresh gunshot wound in the middle of the Atlantic Ocean."

"No," Ben glared briefly, but then he jumped right back in to his story.

"The mirror—I call it a portal—made a small hum as I got closer. It seemed to beckon me. My people tell stories of portals in the past making a way to travel great distances in a short time. According to the old stories, there are principles involved in their use. So I was not afraid of it even though it was my first time to use one. I felt like I knew . . . no, *understood* how to use it." Ben was getting really excited now.

"So I know you might think I'm crazy," he said. (Which we did but offered no judgment at this point as we thought we were crazy too.) "But I went right up to it and stuck my hand in it." He stuck his hand up in the air and stared at it as though it would now reveal something.

"This does sound a bit crazy, Mr. Mosely," Helga said softly and as disarmingly as she could.

"No, this isn't the crazy part," he assured us.

"Oh boy, here we go," I thought to myself. Then, I couldn't help it. I jumped in again. "Is this where the aliens come in!?" I said mocking him while contorting my eyes open as wide as I could force them.

"There are no aliens in this portal I'm telling you about," he replied with disdain and a pout. "I'm telling you what happened to me!"

"Touché. Please *do* go on!" I implored him with a subtle mocking hint in my voice that I'm sure did not escape Helga.

"Anyway, I stuck my hand in it. And it felt very cold, but no harm came to me. So I stuck my head in and looked around. It was another place! I was looking at a snow-covered, windy wilderness." His eyes and face lit up with the memory.

"I was going to go back and get a coat and tell my family, but then I saw a man who looked injured lying in the snow with that Parka on. The one you found me with." He looked at us as though this, the existence of his parka, would be proof and explanation for all of his story.

"So you jumped in!" I exclaimed.

"Yes!" he said as his eyes lit up.

"I jumped in and ran to the man, but he was dead . . . and then I was very cold. So I was going to run back through the portal, but it shimmered and moved away, really fast." He made wild circular motions with his hands to show us how it moved away from him.

"I knew the dead man didn't need the Parka anymore, and I was badly freezing. So I took it off of him and put it on me. Strange thing . . ." he said and looked puzzled.

"Yes, do tell," I said, but, I'll admit, we moved in closer for this part.

"He looked like me. Not identical. But really, really did look like me," he paused for dramatic effect . . . We needed it. Strangely, the hair on my neck raised a little.

"So I took his parka and gloves, and he had some supplies too. I realized I needed them and he didn't. I felt bad, but I didn't want to freeze to death. I took his pants, his boots, snow shoes, everything."

"Did he have any ID?" I broke in.

"No, but the initials in his parka were B.M. like mine!" He smiled the smile of the oblivious.

"What happened next?" Helga broke in.

"A couple of law men showed up and ran towards me. I was scared because of the dead man at my feet and because I took his parka and clothes." He continued, "So I grabbed his little rifle and ran!"

"Ben, you didn't do anything wrong. Why would you do that?" Helga protested.

"I'm a native, so white law men tend to assume the worst . . . and I was standing over a dead body." Ben seemed genuinely sad about this point.

"I'm guessing they shot you then?" I asked.

"No, as I was running, I slipped on a little hill and into a ravine and slid down. Just before I hit the bottom, the rifle flew out of my hands and hit the ground and fired. It got me." Ben hung his head and acted dead for a moment.

"Then, the law men caught up to me. They were standing over me and radioing for help when they saw a man in the distance watching us. They called out to him, 'Hey, what are you doing there!' And he ran off too." Ben smiled at himself over this.

"Why is everyone in your story running from the law?" I furrowed my brows at Ben.

"Just me and some guy in the snow." Pled Ben. "Then the law men yelled at me to stay still and that help was on the way, and they bolted after that guy. I'd listened to the law men talk, and apparently they were out looking for a convict on the lam. Anyway, as I lay in the snow, I could hear the law men running and chasing the man and worse!"

"Worse!" We leaned in again.

"What now?" I asked.

"Wolves!" Ben's voice went up and his expression matched it. "I could hear them in the distance and they were chasing the man and probably the law men too. I knew it wasn't safe to sit there, and I was shot, I was bleeding, and I was getting affected by the extreme cold that I wasn't used to. So I looked up and tried to find somewhere to hide. Then I heard shooting and yelping and a melee off in the distance. More men and wolves must have all caught up. I wasn't sure what to do, and then it appeared again."

"The portal?!" Helga and I cried out in unison.

"Yes, so I crawled to it. I was shaking and vomiting from the cold and from the shooting, but I knew I had to get in it. I used every bit of energy I had left and drug myself across it and . . . wham! I was in your boat."

"Ha ha ha ha . . ." I couldn't contain myself. "That's a ridiculous story," I said, "What am I supposed to think of that? I'm going to turn you over to the authorities as soon as I can find some."

"No, please, believe me!" Ben pled, "I need to call my family and get back to them too."

"Mr. Mosely," Helga joined in, "it is an extravagant tale, and your sudden appearance and the parka and ice on your boots and pants are unexplainable. But I don't know what to think either. All these things just seem very suspicious. You understand this tale is ridiculous don't you?"

Ben put his head down. Then he lifted it up to continue speaking, "I don't know . . ."

At which point everything went amok . . .

I heard an almost melodic hum on deck above me and wild running sounds started above us. "Stay with him," I barked as I left Helga to attend our injured guest, and I burst back up on the deck. Then I found another man with a parka draped around his waist, carrying a medieval sword and shield, running crazed upon the deck, and looking back at a shimmering mirror-like object floating atop the sea beside the ship. He slammed into the ship's mast at full speed and went down hard. Splat!

"That hit actually sounded like the word, 'splat,' " I thought to myself and held back a snort. I started towards him and then the next event unfolded.

The shimmer opened. I heard it vibrate and turned back to it just as a horse with a man upon it started to exit onto the yacht. Apparently, this was what the new guy was running from. Then the shimmer slammed shut loping off the top half of the pursuer as the horse alighted on the deck. Now, I had a horse with a man's bloody lower torso running around the deck and wildly spooked. I also saw an extra sword and shield, presumably from the now loped-apart pursuer, fall through the portal. I picked up the sword (just in case) and tried calming the horse down. He wouldn't have any of it and jumped off the ship into the sea.

The new guy who ran into the mast got up woozily and said something in French (which I don't speak but I can recognize). He turned to a new shimmer, which had materialized over the water on the other side of the boat without me realizing it, and he sprang into the water. He swam to it and splashed through while shouting in English this time, "I'm going home." As he looked back, I noticed that his general facial appearance was quite like my own. "Lucky guy," I laughed at myself. Then I remembered Ben's comparison to his doppelganger in the snow.

At this point, I was standing on the deck in confusion with a medieval sword, a shield, a horse with half of a bloody torso on its saddle swimming around the boat, and questions in my mind about my own sanity.

"Ahoy there boy," I called out to the horse. Helga who was trying to make sure Ben was at peace and resting again arrived back up on deck to see newly spattered blood, medieval weapons, and me look-ing lost and calling to a horse swimming in circles about the boat. Thankfully, the bloody lower torso fell off the horse and floated away before Helga realized what it is. I was also getting concerned that it might attract sharks.

"Have we corporately gone mad?" she said as she looked at me in complete disbelief.

I dropped the sword and kept calling to the horse. "What do you call a male French horse?" I posed to Helga.

She stared at me like I had indeed gone mad and replied, "Beau?"

I called out, "Beau," with my best (worst and fake) French accent, and the horse turned around and started swimming back. In most cases, this would have been a lost cause, but did I mention this was a research vessel? We had all kinds of specially designed platforms and deck access points built on this yacht. I could open a large platform that would let him climb aboard. But I was mulling over how I would I explain that to a French speaking horse.

Meanwhile, Helga had run back to the galley and grabbed a few apples which we held out for the horse to see. When I lowered the access platform with steps, the horse lunged up and came aboard like he'd been trained for it.

"Ok, that went way too easy," I marveled at this turn of events. The horse had calmed down mainly, I think, due to exhaustion from swimming in the sea. Regardless, he let us take his reins and tie him to the ship's support beams.

Now, we needed to find out if Ben could explain any of this.

Of course, Ben had just climbed up on deck too.

"What are you doing up here?" Helga shouted at him, "You should be in bed resting!"

"I'm doing much better," he beamed, "Whose beautiful horse is that?" Ben immediately came over to the horse and started talking to him and petting him. The horse was exhausted from his swim in the Atlantic, but he seemed to respond well to Ben's attention.

We quickly recounted to Ben what had just occurred on deck.

"I don't have any idea about French speaking people," Ben tried to explain, "but this might be a portal crossing area, and that would explain what you've seen."

"Not really," I said, "but it may explain why our benefactor sent us to this precise location. He's been here and seen something. He wants us to see it and help him explain it."

"Or help him use it," said Ben. Then his eyes got huge and lit up as he pointed out to sea.

We spun around to see it. Another shimmering light with a reflective element to it had appeared just over the surface of the water and 25 feet out from the boat.

Ben didn't hesitate, "You've got to take me over to it!" He jumped up and down. "I can go home."

"How do you know that home is where that thing will take you Ben?" I quizzed. At this point, I was starting to believe some parts of this story. What choice did I have? I'd now seen multiple portal appearances all about our ship and random people and animals passing through them without any other explanation.

"Portals come in threes. If you go right in and back, you go back where you started. If you miss the first one and go to a second one, you go to another new location. But if you wait for a third, you can take it back home." Ben explained this like he had a Ph.D. in Portals.

"What about the one that just came with the French horseman?" Helga quizzed.

"I don't think that was my portal because it didn't signal me and just happened here because this does seem to be a portal crossing area."

We were incredulous and filled with more questions after that outburst, but we agreed to help Ben get to the new portal that had opened up. He asked us if he could take the horse because his family had a place for it and he loved horses.

We didn't have horse food or proper disposal systems for him, and I wouldn't for the life of me know how to explain the arrival of the horse to our coming crew or to anyone associated with our scientific work on the yacht (except maybe to our now more mysterious benefactor). So it was easy to say yes to that request. It was a way to bury the evidence, so to speak.

We lowered the horse and Ben via the platform tool again. The horse seemed amazingly willing to go with Ben into the water, and we watched as Ben and the horse swam over to the portal. In they went, and away went our adventure.

"You know we can't ever tell anyone about this crazy event right?" Helga said.

"Yeah, about that, I think I can make a novel out of this experience," I tested her patience, "Plus, I think we ought to be asking our benefactor some more questions."

"We are respectable researchers. I don't want to ruin our reputation."

We turned and looked at the blood, the horse refuse, and the parkas we had to clean up.

"Let's get the mess cleaned up," I said, "Besides, maybe there's a portal out there for us to climb into someday."

The Culling: A Portal Story IV

"The messier it gets, the more I'm convinced we are the righteous."
– Major Bart of the Gavaa'

Blood and guts were everywhere. Nasty Banga Flies were swarming to the scent of the massacre. The sounds of screaming scientist in little white lab coats fleeing scene of the attack filled the air. Thick, acrid smoke with an aroma of melting, plastic-coated electrical wires floated throughout the grounds of the campus, and the echo of small arms fire was all around us. The Gava North Army was running over the main research lab dedicated to portal transportation and other interdimensional contacts. They wanted to end the chance for this Earth's humans to interact with other dimensions once and for all.

The Gava North was now the dominant army and species of this earth. It was a culture of cold-blooded peoples known as the Gavaa'. They had been, centuries earlier, a weak minded subspecies who viewed humans as superiors that they loathed and feared. Now, due to wheat blights and disease, humans were losing ground on our world, and the Gavaa' had gained technical knowledge from us, knowledge that they now used against us. More so, they seemed to be gaining intelligence from previously banned interspecies breeding. There were whispers everywhere that their dynamic and charismatic leader, Supreme Leader Gym Junga, was at best 50% Gavaa' (but 100% cold blooded).

"Hurry John, the G.N.A. will overrun us any minute. Get the research notes and the handheld portal calibrator," shouted Tom.

Tom Tedesco was a man of action, a world traveler and the leading expert on portals in this dimension. He actually wasn't from this dimension, but he had decided to stay years ago when he met, on this Earth, the second Helga Howard he'd known, had fallen in love for the second time, and optimistically decided to help the humans on this Earth revive their flagging existence.

John Josine was Tom's lab assistant at the university and was eager to learn and to help drive forward his people's knowledge and understanding of portals. John quickly tossed Tom the small research notebook and handheld portal calibrators as Tom headed towards a weapons rack.

"John, we don't need those guns. We need to get out of here now!" Tom snarled.

"I'm here now," Helga exclaimed as she came running from down the hall, "I think the G.N.A. are already in this building on floor one. Any portals detected anywhere near us?"

Portals could be found and could be called, but when found naturally, they were more reliable. They'd learned in their studies that when you called a portal, you couldn't initially know where it might take you, and it took time and lots of calculations for Tom to figure out how to get another to take you back to the point of origin.

Tom turned on one of the calibrators, "Yes, thankfully, one in the jungle to the south. Let's get to the Jungle Rover, out the back side of the building."

"Tom, there will be G.N.A. there watching by now," John cautioned.

"I have a flash bomb in my lab coat from my last trip to what I call Earth-22. They make good defensive weapons there, and the

Gavaa' are very sensitive to light," Tom giggled with glee at the advantage he felt he had.

Tom, Helga, and John all raced to the back side stairs and gathered at the exit door. They paused for a moment to catch their breath and listened to hear any movement outside the door. Everything was quiet on this side of the building, and they couldn't hear anything at all from the other side of the door.

"I didn't think it would be that quiet on this side, but anyway, I parked the rover about 100 feet straight out this door yesterday to get ready. Put on your sunglasses. John, you open the door. I'll take a quick look and throw the flash bomb if I see any trouble," Tom barked out his orders.

John grabbed the door and braced for action. He flung it open and two Gavaa' troops immediately fell in on the group! The Gavaa' had been waiting at the back door and holding their breath to keep quiet.

Squealing with delight, the incredibly strong Gavaa' were overpowering Tom and John as they wrestled in the doorway and hall until Tom heard the sounds of relief.

The electrifying sounds of bzzts and zaps crackled as Helga applied a stun gun that she kept in her lab coat to the back of the Gavaa'. The Gavaa' don't generally view female humans as a threat. To their detriment, they focused solely on Tom and John and left Helga free to subdue them with the stun gun from behind.

"Thanks Helga! I'm sure glad the Gavaa' are so prejudiced," John exclaimed with joy.

"They'll learn whether they want to or not," Helga glared.

"Let's get to the rover before more get here," Tom was spitting out, but all three were already moving that way. They could hear rushing movement coming from the side of the building behind them, but they dove into the rover and powered it on. Tom had thought long ago to install bullet proof glass in all viewpoints on the rover. It could handle small arms fire which is the typical weapon of Gavaa' troops.

"Let's knock a few Gavaa' senseless as we go," Tom could barely contain himself. The powerful torque of the hybrid electric rover was very responsive and quick in small spaces. He pulled the rover into position from where he could blast down a jungle trail and threw the flash bomb out his window into a group of six Gavaa' troopers. The bomb lit up the clearing and knocked the Gavaa' to the ground in temporary blindness. He rushed the rover down the jungle trail and towards the portal signal his calibrator had picked up.

Tom's research and refinement of the portal calibrators was the stuff of legends on Hanna' (this new Earth he had adopted). Tom had been an electrical engineer with a specialty in radio wave transmission back on his earth. In fact, it was that work on his home earth that led him to discover the waves of energy that portals send out when they come and go. Further, his research led to the understanding of the way portals directed themselves across dimensions and space. While not perfectly, he could predict their appearance, call them, and direct them within a reasonable margin of error (but a margin of error slightly larger than Tom could account for in a purely mathematical model). There were errors along the way that made the portals seem at times almost intentional in their variances from his calculations, variances that backed up the old legends about living portals. His work was still a work in progress. He'd done most of his research on the calibrators after arriving on Hanna'. The human population was small enough that he felt safe developing it with them, not like on his own earth where he feared the massive government bureaucracy would snap up, steal, and weaponize his research. Further, the humans of Hanna' needed his help, and the dominant human government of Cravea had granted him labs, research tools, help, and funding. They viewed Tom as the best chance to save the humans of Cravea—and all Hanna'—from the continually encroaching Gavaa'.

As the rover sped away, a larger contingent of Gavaa' canvassed the research campus, and Major Bart arrived. Major Bart was favored by Gym Junga and had a penchant for using human phrasing and sarcasm, something the Gavaa' struggled with, as he brutally slaughtered humans at the fronts of the continuing land grabs by the Gavaa'.

"The messier it gets, the more I'm convinced we are the righteous," Major Bart of the Gavaa' exclaimed in glee as he unloaded from a motorcycle his troops had scavenged from the humans of Hanna' at some point in the recent past.

His troops and their sergeant looked at him with the understanding of a dodo bird, a species which had flourished on Hanna'. Apparently, the dodos here could bite very aggressively in defense, and that's all they needed to survive (as opposed to their Earth cousins).

Major Bart grinned the toothy grin of the Gavaa'. "We shall overcome these arrogant humans. They are weak and greedy. They want to hoard all knowledge for themselves. Follow their trail. But if you catch up to them, cut them off. Don't try diving after them if they find a portal."

Sergeant Galon barked out orders to the troops who quickly mounted magna speeders that could easily catch up to the rover. He'd carefully (for a Gavaa') instructed them not to chase the portal scientists into a portal. "It will give them an advantage over you," he'd warned. But he knew at least one would disobey. "They think they are being brave when they chase their prey. But they are being stupid, and they all will learn from the stupid actions of the rash one. Major Barttt," he said, struggling with such a human name, "one will lose an appendage or his life in the chase." At this pronouncement, he grinned at Major Bart.

"Yes, they must learn that Gavaa' do not chase prey . . . We stalk them, corner them, and defeat them," Major Bart sneered back.

Tom had chosen the rover for several reasons. He could haul more people and equipment and modify it to be bullet proof, and it was more muscular in heavy jungle conditions. The head start they had on the pursuing troops should be enough to get them to the portal they'd located before the troops could close on them.

"How much longer Tom?" Helga queried nervously.

"We should be on it in five minutes or less," Tom smiled to reassure Helga.

Helga was rubbing the stun gun in her hand for comfort like it was a pet or a medicine stick. To Tom's chagrin, John had grabbed a few handguns and was making sure they were loaded.

"I'm all for self-defense John, but don't use those unless you have to. We're no different from the Gavaa' if you just kill them because they don't like you." Tom was not a pacifist, but he knew his image among the Gavaa' mattered. They held Tom in a kind of awe as they'd seen how he could command and summon portals. Tom continued, "They need a better model than the one of mayhem and destruction they are using to take over Hanna' from the human population."

"I won't shoot them because I don't like them. I'll shoot them because I don't want them to shoot me first," John lightly glared. Then he trailed off, attempting light humor with a small grin, and said, ". . . and I don't really like them . . ."

They all chuckled a bit at John's attempt. Up ahead was a clearing, and a portal could be seen at the far end of it, maybe 300 yards out.

"We've got it!" shouted John.

They stopped to unload and make a run for it, about a hundred feet from the shimmering, glassy, beautiful portal that would be their escape. But as they exited, Tom stopped, frozen, and pointed. Then Gavaa' mounted speeders burst out of the jungle ahead of them and behind them, cutting off their access to the portal.

"Spit and venom," John sprayed out the words at the edge of this mouth, "Those magna speeders are so fast and quiet as a mouse. I thought we had them beaten."

"We're going to try something quickly," Tom barked out orders as he tossed the second calibrator to John, "That one is set to call the portal. I'm trying to dial this one into the Southern edge of Cravea . . ." His words trailed off as he saw how quickly the troops were closing. He knew he wouldn't have time for that much calculation.

The speeder mounted troops had unmounted and were starting to close on the portal voyagers as John fired his calibrator towards the portal. Gavaa' troops fired on them in response, but the portal shimmered and burst in between the two groups. They ran to cover the forty feet left to the portal as it fixed its location in front of them, and they dove forward.

The Gavaa' troops rushed to go around to the other side of the portal and cut them off, but as the closest trooper closed in on them, a nest of dodo birds hidden in the grass jumped out and bit his legs. As he fell, the next closest Gavaa' rushed past and cut around the edge of the portal.

Too late the humans were in!

"No!" shouted Gavaa' trooper Bragg Mosely. The portal's tone shifted as he charged forward to chase the escaping travelers. "You will not escape me. I am Bragg Mosely, a Gavaa' of Hanna', and you will not . . ." His words were drowned out from the humming of the portal as he dove with his right arm and pistol, leading into the buzzing portal.

"Halt, Bragg Mosely!" shouted his sergeant.

The sergeant knew he was barking his order in vain. There was no stopping Bragg Mosely's surge forward. The portal shimmered and shut as Bragg's arm went in. "Thud," went Bragg's body as his arm was loped off, and he collapsed into the ground where the portal once shimmered.

On the other side of the portal, the travelers materialized at once. They were inside a house, in what appeared to be a den with a cat sleeping in a chair. Clomp! . . . The arm of the Gavaa' trooper fell through as they all turned around to see the portal evaporate.

"Where are we?" said Helga.

"I had auto calibrated for us to end up on my Earth at a college in Tulsa if I was ever in a bind," Tom replied, "But portals tend to go and end where recent portals on the same Earth have been. Tulsa is a crossroads for portals, so this one just ended in someone's house."

"Mine," came the gravely and grim voice of a man holding a shotgun aimed at them. "Who are you?" he demanded.

The travelers studied their unexpected and unwelcoming host thoroughly. He had a color-drained look like he was seeing ghosts. Yet there was something uncomfortably odd and familiar about him. He was older than Tom and a little shorter, but he was Tom's twin or nearly so! Then they saw his companion, a blonde-haired woman with a trim, solid figure, and she was familiar too! Now the color was draining out of the travelers' faces.

"Who are you?" repeated the man with the shotgun.

"I'm Tom Tedesco—world traveler," said Tom in a calm if slightly unnerved voice, "and this is John Josine and Helga Howard Tedesco."

"The . . . what . . . I'm Tom Tedesco, and she's Helga!!!" shouted the man with the shotgun, pointing at his companion. Even as he said it, this older version of Tom seemed to be grasping at what was happening. That was until he saw the Gavaa' arm.

"What are you doing with that arm I just buried last evening down in the ravine?!" was his next question.

"Tom, I don't think that's the same dead arm wriggling on the floor. It just came off the body of a Gavaa' warrior who tried to chase us into the portal. They're a cold blooded species, and they can re-grow limbs. So he'll likely be ok," Tom Tedesco of Hanna' reasoned aloud.

"You're portal travelers like us," came the voice of older Helga with wide blue eyes.

"Yes," said younger Helga, "and we just portaled in. Are we safe here?"

"Yes," said older Helga, "Tom, put down the shotgun."

Tom complied, and the tension in the room eased. The travelers spent the next ten minutes giving a quick rundown of their history. They agreed older Tom would be called Thomas and Tom would be Tom. Older Helga would be Henny, a childhood nickname that apparently both Helgas had been given in grade school, to keep confusion down. Thomas and Henny gave a brief history of their two portal travels up to this point, including the most recent when they'd had to hide a severed arm in a ravine in the nearby woods for fear of police they'd sent away. They weren't as experienced as the travelers, but both Tom and Thomas seemed to have an almost common grasp of how portals worked and why the travelers' portal had unloaded them there, in the den of Thomas and Henny.

Thud, Thud. There came a pounding at the front door.

The temporary peace in the room ended.

"Who's that?" The travelers asked in unison.

Henny and Thomas looked at each other in terror.

"It can't be the police can it?" Henny's eyes pleaded with Thomas for reassurance.

"I don't know. I'll go look. Please get them a black plastic trash bag from the kitchen for that arm, and get some hydrogen peroxide to clean that blood." Thomas spat out orders as he headed to the door. Helga noted the similarity in the Tom's abilities to tell others what to do.

Thomas let out a sigh of relief as he looked through the peephole. It was only his neighbor, squirrely, annoying Ben Mosely. "It's just Ben Mosely everyone!" Thomas smiled back.

The travelers tensed at the name. Tom was going to ask for a pause, but it was too late. Thomas had opened the door. Ben held up his right arm and then suddenly yanked it off. His right arm was a prosthetic!

"Give me the arm," Ben demanded, "I am a Dagor of Hanna', and I need the arm for a healing catalyst to my own damaged arm." He demanded it, but he said it flatly and didn't threaten anything.

Thomas, stunned, stood in the doorway, and then Tom broke the silence. "He won't harm us," Tom announced, "The Dagor are biological cousins of the Gavaa', and the Dagor always seem to have a biological sensor for blood and for the Gavaa'. This Ben Mosely is connected to the Gavaa' warrior we knew, like each of us is connected, but he is not the same."

"May I please have the arm," his tone had softened. But he was desperately pushing forward, so Thomas let him in and closed the door. Ben rushed to the arm, pulled out a knife, and cut slices in the arm's end and his own remaining arm stub. He shoved them together and then used his own tee shirt to bind them up.

The travelers and Thomas were stunned by the macabre arm-repair operation that Ben the Dagor had performed as calmly as though it were just a meal he was preparing for dinner.

"This will reactivate my arm's natural healing process!" Ben Moseley the Dagor beamed.

Thud! Thud!

"Is this the most popular house on the block?" John Josine attempted weakly to lighten the sudden tension exuding from Thomas and Henny. Henny had just arrived back in the den with a black trash bag, peroxide, and cleaning rags to find her neighbor, Ben Mosely, who was looking like a hospital patient, standing with a severed arm wrapped against his own body, and hovering over a pool of severed-arm blood.

Thomas went to the door again. "Oh CRAP! It is the police this time. Well . . . it's just one. He has what looks like a warrant . . . and I know him?" Tom said with a question mark on his face as he opened the door partially to say hello.

"Sheriff Thompson! Hello," Thomas bellowed out as he smiled and stepped out onto the entryway with the sheriff he knew.

Then, it all broke loose.

Two cops hiding behind the bushes leapt between Tom and the door, ripped open his door, and flew in.

"Hey stop!" yelled Thomas.

"Stop!" yelled Sheriff Thompson, and in they all flew. The police were pulling guns on everyone, even the Sheriff, as he came up yelling at them from behind Tom. The travelers were standing together with Ben and Helga. Blood was all over the floor. Ben's reattached arm looked black and putrid and was clearly not perfectly reattached to his body. The two policemen seemed overwhelmed and angry. Tom hit the call button on his portal calibrator discreetly.

Then, everyone, including the police, froze as a large, shimmering, and liquid mirror hummed into existence and appeared behind the travelers. The travelers knew what to do. They fell backwards into the shimmer as they'd done tens of times before, and Ben went right with them.

Then the policemen were totally and completely confused. They were in a stunned stupor, staring back and forth at Thomas and Henny and the portal while Sheriff Thompson was trying to gain their attention. Thomas and Henny hesitated, glanced at each other, and dove in backwards as the two police started to argue between themselves about jumping in and following the travelers into the portal.

"Don't attempt to chase them!" the Sheriff barked out a warning as though he knew about portals. Thomas heard it as he was falling in, and he saw one of the policemen stick in a leg as he stepped forward in pursuit.

As Thomas and Henny joined the travelers, half a severed leg fell in behind them.

"You can push that back through," said Tom, but he bent over grabbed it as blood was starting to spurt out of it and pushed it back through himself.

"Can we ever go back to our life on our earth again?" Henny was trying to grasp the overwhelming set of events that had just occurred.

"Yes," Thomas reassured her, "Sheriff Thompson knows about portals and knows we did nothing wrong. We can defend ourselves, if needed, in court. But it's pretty intense over there right now I imagine, so let's allow them to settle down. They'll be focusing on care for the policeman with the severed leg. We'll go back later."

"And where is here?" Henny marveled as she looked around. They were in a cavern that needed exploring, and they had no supplies, as opposed to the last time when they carried more than they could bear. She needn't worry as the travelers from Hanna' had carried plenty of supplies, including, most importantly, two flashlights.

"I don't know yet," said Tom, "but I can calibrate it in about two hours. So stay close while I work this out. And where's your neighbor Ben? I didn't see him come through." Everyone looked around, but Ben was gone.

"He may have been affected differently by the portal due to his unique DNA and thus sent sideways to a dimension or location more in line with his background," Tom was positing things he didn't really know as though he did to try to settle down both Helgas now.

"One thing's for sure, we are back on Hanna," Helga pointed to cave drawings on the wall, "Those are Gavaa' drawings." There were drawings of their dreams and plans all over the massive cave walls. She panned up with her flashlight, and a story took shape. The early Gavaa' had recorded the humiliating defeats they'd suffered over the years to early humans. Though humans had grown more compassionate towards the Gavaa' centuries ago, the Gavaa' had not forgotten the atrocities. Worse, their plan to conquer the planet was laid out in excruciating detail on the ancient, dry cavern walls. This plan included the spreading of disease to weaken humans before a final push to annihilate them from the planet. They were following a plan, a plan for culling the world of all humans. It was a well written plan, and it was unfolding all around them now.

"How did they get the know how to weaponize disease against humans?" Helga gasped out.

"I have a theory for that," Thomas posited, "Gavaa' are not the only cold-blooded humanoids in the multiple dimensions connected by the Portals. I've met a few before."

A chill ran down every spine in the room.

From behind them, up in a hole within the walls of the cavern, a Dagor named Ben Mosely was watching. "I know where they got it from," Ben cackled softly to himself. His left eye twitched the twitch of an all-knowing Dagor Lord. Then he sang to himself softly the justification poems of his ancestors, *"The messier it gets, the more I'm convinced we are the righteous."*

"Hsst . . . ha, yes, we are righteous. Yes we are . . ." and with that, Ben slunk back into the darkness of the caverns. He knew the way to the stronghold of Gym Junga. He'd be there with fresh news in half a day.

Swamped: A Portal Story V

"What did I have to drink?" Warden Halverson moaned. "A knock on the head by a tree limb," Tom stated, *"I'd offer another, but I don't have the ingredients anymore."*

He leapt from a perch forty feet up in the trees and crashed down upon his prey. As he fell upon and crushed it, he snapped the neck of the first hapless deer that had wandered under his treehouse in six weeks. Blood flowed from the deer's nose, and Gerard Gunga knew that his dinner would be delectable. Despite the alligators, mosquitos, and flies all about him, Gerard was very much at peace in the dense Louisiana bayou. The alligators moved away in deference when he came near, and the mosquitos and flies wouldn't land on him as they were repelled by the smell of his glands.

You see, Gerard was a Gavaa' offspring from another dimension who had been abandoned and matured alone here on Earth. The Gavaa' are a cold-blooded humanoid that competed with humans on an alternate earth. Their external appearance is relatively human but a lot more like a Neanderthal from our world (wide-bodied and thick-limbed), and they are a stout and strong people. Where they differ from humans is their lizard-like DNA. They can lose and re-grow limbs. They have very little hair on the surface of their dark ruddy skin, and they like to eat raw meat. If they laid eggs (and they don't), you might call them the duck-billed platypus of their planet.

While Gerard was crunching down his fresh dinner in large rips of raw venison flesh, a shimmering, liquid mirror of light, which Gerard recognized as a portal, vibrated into existence in the humid Louisiana bayou that Gerard now called home. Out of the portal walked a man who brought to mind bad memories, Tom Tedesco, carrying a sword. Gerard didn't know why because he hadn't actually ever met Tom (or any other person) in his short existence. Gerard was only nine months old.

"Bad!!" Gerard roared at Tom.

I previously mentioned that Gavaa' can regrow limbs, but an abandoned Gavaa' limb can regrow a body too. When a large enough Gavaa' appendage is cleanly severed, it will grow into a new Gavaa' in several stages. Gavaa' who develop from the appendage of another Gavaa' have about half the memories of the predecessor and all the instincts. This allows Gavaa' crawlings (as they are known) to survive on their own from the time of severing. With the predecessor's memories, they can speak once the severed limb develops its full body structure, including vocal cords. The speech of a new Gavaa' crawling may be awkward at times until they have exercised the muscles necessary to utilize the vocabulary they remember.

Startled but in control, Tom responded, "Do I know you?" He took in the full picture as he looked Gerard up and down. Here was what appeared to be a full-sized, adult Gavaa' warrior with deer remains about him and blood all over his face. "Gaak! He's eating it raw!" he thought as he sucked in all the available oxygen around him and wondered at the sight of Gerard. He held his sword up to check any potential advance.

Tom was a regular portal traveler now. His first experience was in the arctic when he used a portal to escape pursuit by a pack of wolves. He'd been to medieval France and stayed there nearly a year. He'd been to a jungle-like world that he didn't believe was even on Earth and had learned about the Gavaa' and the Dagor there. Now, here he was, hoping he was home only to find a Gavaa' pointing at him in condemnation.

"You cut my father's arm off and buried it in the woods!" Gerard stood to size up Tom.

The problem was that this wasn't the Tom Tedesco that had previously run into Gerard's predecessor. Gerard had grown on Earth from the severed arm of a Gavaa' named Major Bart. Major Bart had attempted to chase an older Tom and Helga Tedesco (we'll explain that later), who were of this world, through a portal from Major Bart's earth (a world called Hannah). Portals will snap shut and lop off an appendage on a predator chasing prey through a portal, and that is exactly what happened to Major Bart. For Major Bart, this happened twenty years ago, but as portals can move people through time as well as space, this was only nine months ago for Gerard.

"I'm afraid you have me at a loss," Tom responded strongly and waved the sword at Gerard.

"I see now that you are not the man that my father met. You are younger than the man that my father chased into a portal," Gerard was assessing Tom's demeanor and remembering as much as he could about his father's encounter, "but you smell bad just like him." Gerard turned his nose up to reflect his feelings regarding Tom and his entrance into the bayou.

"He must have been a sweet guy!" Tom replied.

"No!" Gerard was pacing and roaring about now. Though he was only nine months old (the length of time it takes a well-fed Gavaa' arm to regrow into a humanoid body), he now stood six feet tall and was itching to take on a human. Meanwhile, Tom was assessing whether to jump backwards into the portal behind him or to take on the Gavaa' in front of him. There was a mild hum and vibration, and then the portal evaporated.

"I guess that eliminates option number one. Why don't we talk a bit my bloody Gavaa' warrior? Perhaps we can help each other?" Tom felt he could defend himself, but he wanted to learn what this Gavaa' knew of the world they were in.

"Why should I help you?" Gerard blasted his words out.

"Because I can help you get back to your home world and your father," Tom was making an educated guess that this Gavaa' came from the world he'd just left, "You come from Hannah don't you?"

Gerard snorted a bit and picked up a large tree limb that he could use as a bat for Tom's head. "Yes, my father is from Hannah, but I am Gerard. And I grew here from the remains of my father's severed arm. How can you help me get to Hannah?" As a nine-month-old with the memories of a twenty-two-year-old, his acting wasn't great. While Tom was ruminating on the image and implications of a severed arm from Hannah growing into a full sized Gavaa' warrior in nine months, it was obvious to Tom that Gerard wanted to know how to get to his home world of Hannah and to his father, Major Bart.

Tom had heard of the Gavaa' regrowth ability, but he hadn't actually met a Gavaa' crawling in his short time on Hannah. "How old are you, who raised you here, and what do you know about portals?"

"I raised myself after crawling out of the grave another man buried me in. I crawled to the river where I could obtain nourishment and floated to this bayou. I think I am about nine months old, but I have my father's adult memories to teach me . . . or most of them." Then he snarled and burst out with, "But I want to know about portal travel! How can I get to Hannah!" Patience is not a strong suit for the Gavaa'.

"Yes, I see," Tom was mildly amused with having to deal with a nine-month-old Gavaa' warrior in a full man's body, "You know that natural portals come in threes don't you? Or didn't your daddy's memories help you there?"

"Yes, I know!" Gerard was lying, but he didn't want to seem naïve, "What else?" He had stopped pacing and was listening to Tom intently now.

"The first and third are tied to the same location. You just saw me come in number one, and I did come from Hannah. That means we have to watch for number three in this area to get you back to Hannah."

"Why do you help me . . . ?" Gerard was unsure of whether to trust Tom's offers of help. He had rehearsed memories of social interactions, but, in his first nine months of existence, this was the first actual conversation he'd had with a person of any kind.

"You don't really belong on this planet, and you do belong on Hannah," Tom was guessing and half hoping this was true. If Gerard didn't belong here, maybe here was Tom's earth after all.

Then a stunning interjection in their conversation occurred.

The local game warden, Brad Halverson, showed up. "I don't suppose you have a license for that sword do you sir?" Brad liked to break the ice with dry humor. It didn't always work.

Gerard threw the large tree limb in his hand at the warden's head, and it connected with a sickening crack not unlike the sound of a bowling ball hitting a tile counter as opposed to the hardwood floor of the bowling alley. Down went the warden.

"Oh crap Gerard, now we'll be hounded by other law men until they find us!" Tom cried out.

"Not if we find portal" Gerard grunted out disgusting chuckle sounds. He was very proud of his direct hit on the head of warden Halverson.

"First off, portals are very unreliable from a timing perspective. Secondly, if we don't get you in one quickly, you'll be a Guinea pig here for the government to study. Let's get him disarmed and tied up before he comes to . . ." Tom's voice trailed off, and he was looking over the warden when he saw it. There was a rat-like tattoo on the back of his neck. The hair on the back of Tom's neck responded accordingly. "I've seen that exact tattoo before on my earth, so surely that is a sign that this is my world?" he pondered to himself.

Then the other shoe dropped. Tom heard a hum behind him. He knew a portal was forming, but this one sounded different than the norm. And it was. This portal was not a natural portal and was being controlled by newly obtained technology. It came with a harmonic hum, loud popping sounds like an electrical transformer going out, and a dissonant hum. It also came with what was (for Tom) an unwanted guest. As it shimmered into existence, a powerful presence stepped forth. It was the Gavaa' warrior Tom had been running from on Hannah.

"Major Bart, my heart beats with excited palpitations for you," Tom feigned his admiration for the Gavaa' warrior who stepped forth from the shimmering portal, but Tom's frock was now sopping with sweat.

Tom was relieved to discover that he was not the focus of Major Bart's attention. Major Bart carried the presence of a mighty warrior and strode out of the portal directly towards Gerard. Gerard squealed a disgusting sound of Gavaa' glee and rushed to his father. They performed a kind of ritual greeting with chest bumping and head butting and then turned to go back into the newly manufactured portal gateway together. "Tonight we sing the song of the righteous my son, for one who was lost is now found," Major Bart liked to sound eloquent when he took command of a situation.

Major Bart stopped and looked with disgust at Tom. "Do not come back to Hannah again traveler, or it will be your last visit. I spare you this once because you led me to my crawling son. Besides, your days are numbered now. We Gavaa' have new allies in our battles." With that, he and Gerard were off and back to Hannah, and Tom was left with an unconscious deputy and a decision to make.

"Do I try to explain this or just leave him here and run? And what did Major Bart mean about 'your days are numbered now?' I barely had any encounters with him." The choices started to spill out of his mind and into his mouth in loud babblings, "Oh crap, oh crap. What now? Run? Stay? Hide?"

"I'd say hide, but you're way too flamboyant with that medieval French frock and sword outfit you have going on." Startled, Tom looked back to see a skinny, beautiful brunette had appeared. Strangely, here she was in the middle of a Louisiana swamp dressed in business attire, with a classic skirt, a no-frill dress shirt, a vest, and high heels.

His heart raced due to the startling appearance of the woman, and his tongue failed him for a moment as his jaw dropped open.

"I know, I'm pretty amazing for a girl with a gun pointed on you." She smiled as she made the weapon she held a little more visible in the moonlight. "Can you explain why you have the game warden unconscious at your feet?"

Tom gathered his thoughts as quickly as he could, "Where's a good portal when you need one?" He grasped at options to explain. "A large bigfoot creature clubbed him with that limb?" came out.

"Hmm, hmm," a light snickering came out from the thin figure of the woman who stood before him. "So we start with lies?"

"She has a sense of humor," he thought as he felt a glimmer of hope. "Actually, he was hit in the head by an interdimensional warrior child before his father appeared in a manufactured teleportation portal and took him away." He laughed at himself now as he knew she'd never go for that.

"Oh, a Dagor?" She replied with total acceptance of that possibility.

"No, a Gavaa' warrior." Tom wondered if she was drinking or confused about the pronunciation of the Gavaa'.

"Oh yes, the Dagor have told me of the less developed Gavaa' civilization from Hannah, but they aren't supposed to have portal tech yet." She made a concerned pause, almost like she was calculating the implications of Gavaa' warriors with portal control tech." Then she snapped back to Tom's gaze, "Again, why is the warden on the ground?"

"I'll pick him up," and with that, Tom put his sword in his scabbard and picked up the officer to carry him, "Where are we going? And who are you?"

"We're going to my house to clean him up, and I'm Melanie Scarab," said the brunette, "And you?"

"Tom Tedesco," Tom replied.

Melanie smiled a knowing smile. "Of course you are," she said as she turned and headed down a slight trail that Tom had not previously noticed in the wooded bayou.

A few short minutes later, they were at Melanie's stunningly luxuriant mansion in the bayou. There was a massive front porch with colonial columns. The furniture looked like it came from the castle of a European monarch. Tom was trying to understand what he'd walked into as the warden started to come to. "What did I have to drink?" Warden Halverson moaned.

"A knock on the head by a tree limb," Tom stated, "I'd offer another, but I don't have the ingredients anymore."

Halverson recognized Melanie's home as he gathered himself. "What exactly was going on down there? And who are you?" he questioned Tom.

"I'm Tom Tedesco," then Tom thought better of giving any details.

Melanie stunned Tom with a sudden revelation, "Tom, he knows about portal travels. It's ok to reveal who you are and what you know to Brad." Now Tom was the one who was trying to reorient himself.

"Ok, you got me Melanie. Who are you, and how do you know about portals and me? And why does Brad have a rat tattoo on his neck?" Tom was actually a bit irritated at being the one in the room who was not sure where he was. After all, he hadn't been hit on the head by a tree limb (at least not yet).

"I'm Melanie Scarab, as I said before, and I'm one of the keepers of the portals on this world. I'm a gatekeeper really. We have our defenders spread around the world in various known portal crossing areas, and we try to keep them safe and those who use them safe as well. We also try to defend and keep various versions of earth safe from invasion, particularly for those human civilizations who've yet to master and integrate portal travel into their culture. The rat tattoo is a symbol for the specific company here on earth that work for a military force that supports the gatekeepers and defend the portals. They are referred to collectively as The Hawks. There are many protectors of the portals, Tom. Those like me are the hands of our organization, and the tattooed soldiers are the arms."

That was a bit much for Tom to swallow, "I've been portal traveling for almost two years now. Where were your people to keep me safe when I jumped from the arctic tundra to medieval France or from there to the planet Hannah or into your swamp tonight where I had to defend myself from a Gavaa warrior." Tom was overwhelmed and lost himself in his own soliloquy.

Melanie laughed a disarming laugh, "Tom you are with friends. You just don't know it yet. We know you peripherally at least because there is a Tom Tedesco on almost every planet we've crossed, and, in fact, our group was formed by a Tom Tedesco many years ago. You seem to be natural adventurers and often have an engineering or science background that helps you gain control or at least effectiveness in your use of the portal network. On some planets we meet more than one Tom Tedesco, and there are presently at least two from this earth."

"I need to lay down," Tom groaned as he found his way to a chair on which to rest for a moment, "I have to absorb all this, you know."

"Yes, I imagine so," Melanie said as she seemed to feign understanding, "Go upstairs. Take a shower. There are spare clothes for a man of your size in the third room on the left which can serve as your guest bedroom tonight."

Tom was too tired to argue, and he went up to take the first modern shower he'd had in a year and to get a full night of sleep.

The next morning Tom awoke to "Tom get up." Melanie had come in to rustle Tom back into the world.

"Oh crap," Tom realized he hadn't been dreaming, "you mean you and your revelations are all real?"

"Hmm . . . yes Tom, I'm real, and everything I told you last night is still true. More importantly, you need to get back to the swamp."

"Why the rush?" Tom raised his eyebrow at Melanie.

"Two more portals that you missed came last night in the swamp, which is fine because the first was to Africa and the second was back to Hannah. I think you're ready to go home for a time, and you're needed there. So if you don't want to hitchhike back to the arctic, you need to catch the next one. It's your ticket back."

"Am I on the right earth now?" Tom questioned.

"Yes, but in Louisiana, not up north," Melanie replied, "But more importantly, your home is about to be attacked, and you need to get home to defend it."

"What? By who? And how do you know that?"

"We have spies and portal keepers Tom. Your cabin will shortly be under attack by Dagor who've determined that anyone named Tom Tedesco is a threat to their plans for domination of the portal network. So I'm sending Brad Halverson to help protect you, and our network has already sent a small company of soldiers to your cabin to protect you. But it will look good if you're there to show support."

"Let's go," Tom was up and gathering his sword.

As he met her downstairs, he noticed that Melanie was in a fresh outfit that was nearly identical to the one she'd worn the night before. "It's like she was dressed to go to court in the 1980s," Tom thought, wondering about any significance there.

Back at the swamp, Tom was getting impatient, "Are we in the right area?"

Brad and Melanie both had a very large weapon, which looked like a cross between a rifle and an air gun, strapped to their backs. Brad also had a small bag the size of a child's school backpack with him. Melanie had in her hands what looked like a portable GPS but which was apparently a piece of portal locator tech.

"Yes Tom, and it's three minutes away." Melanie responded.

Then it happened again; Tom heard the harmonic and dissonant humming and the snapping of the artificial portal that Major Bart had used last night. He whirled around to watch it form. Before the portal could unload its travelers, Melanie and Brad were firing their weapons into it. "Apparently, they know the difference between a natural and an artificial portal too" Tom observed to himself.

But the unseen enemy apparently had prepared for this. Two more artificial portals were opening around them, and they couldn't maintain fire on all three portals simultaneously. A group of Gavaa' warriors jumped out of one portal and rolled into the bayou woods for cover.

"We need backup," Tom shouted, "do you have more?"

"Yes, but they are at your place. This is a distraction." Brad shouted back.

Then the natural portal that Tom had been waiting on appeared just behind him. He looked at his new companions to see how they intended to proceed, but it was obvious that Brad was coming and Melanie was planning to stay.

"Come with me," Tom urged Melanie. Then Brad grabbed him and pulled hard, and they fell backwards into the portal.

As they came out on the other side, they were in an arctic environment (Tom's cabin was nearby), and the portal shimmered and evaporated. Instantaneously, Brad popped a release valve on the little backpack he had brought, and it expanded like a helium balloon being filled at the fair. It ruptured and released two parkas and arctic gear which they needed and donned in short shrift.

"Why did you abandon Melanie back there?" Tom was irked with Brad for grabbing him and leaving Melanie.

"It's her post there, and she's fine. That assault was to stop you from getting here. They'll abandon her now that we've made it, but we need to get to your cabin right away."

"You sure they wouldn't take her as a hostage?"

"Yes, they wouldn't have any use for a Melanie." Brad smiled with a strange kind of smirk, and then pointed in the direction that his GPS said to head. They turned to the northeast and ran towards Tom's cabin. It was still a snowy environment, but this was late spring, and the snow had cleared quite a bit so the way to the cabin was not overly challenging. In minutes they arrived and found the company of about eighty soldiers ready to protect Tom and his cabin.

Then a hail storm of action broke out. A dozen portals opened and unloaded both Dagor and Gavaa' warriors. A strike was made on a small communications tower the company had set up. Tom was quickly handed one of their oversized, rifle-like weapons which he quickly discovered was a form of shoulder mounted, quick burst laser cannon. The soldier who handed it to Tom said, "Check the power gauge from time to time, but the essence of the shoulder cannon is aim and shoot."

The company of Tom's defenders were slightly outnumbered, but they took to the fight with great efficiency. Still, Tom felt every bit of the stress of combat as the enemy was closing in on them. Gavaa' warriors were the most aggressive of the attackers, constantly charging from different angles, but they were also taking the most losses. The Dagor on the other hand, while more conservative in their attacks, were using the Gavaa' attacks to set up the Hawks for sniping. The Hawks had anticipated being surrounded and, to Tom's surprise, had laid radio-controlled mines around the perimeter. They were just waiting for the Dagor fighters to get to the right place, and then they pulled the trigger. Explosions rocked the woods around the cabin, and the Dagor and Gavaa' decided to retreat for a better assault opportunity. And with that, it was over as quickly as it had started.

"We're clear for a while," said Brad.

"How will we know when they might come back?" Tom questioned Brad, ". . . and how will we defend ourselves when they bring twice as many next time?"

"Leave military planning to the military people," Brad replied, "We know what we're doing. Now I have to get a message off to my higher-ups. They need to know the Gavaa' have joined the Dagor empire."

"Ok, and when you get back, you still have to explain what you meant when you said they wouldn't have any use for a Melanie!"

He spoke too late as Brad had hightailed it to a new communications tent that the defenders of Tom's cabin had set up.

Seconds later, Brad showed up with a message and a flushed face, "Tom, your wife and kids inside the cabin are insisting you come in and see them. We haven't let them out since we arrived."

"That's a problem Brad. You see, this certainly looks like my cabin, but I don't have a wife and kids." Tom tried a little humor, "Have you been hitting me with Gerard's tree limb when I've been looking away?"

"No sir, now I'm concerned. Who are they . . ." And when that question had barely escaped Brad's lips, Tom's cabin exploded. It blew up with a massive display of wood, sparks, and debris. Many of the company near the cabin were killed, injured, or at minimum knocked to the ground depending on their proximity to it. Tom and Brad were far enough to the edge of the grounds that they sustained only a temporary loss of hearing, and a ringing sound persisted in their ears for a few minutes.

Tom and Brad gathered themselves and immediately started helping the wounded.

"Who did that?" Tom was stunned, but the fact that he'd seen enough bizarre things recently seemed to inoculate him from going completely into shock.

"Your wife and kids?" Brad suggested with a sarcastic tone, "On most worlds I've been to, Tom Tedescoes are married to Helga Howard Tedescoes. The persons or things in that cabin looked like most of them."

"You've got to be kidding me," Tom seemed amazed at the prospect, "You mean on all the other worlds you're aware of with a Tom

Tedesco he's, or they've, been married to women with a certain name? I never met a woman on this world that I connected with in that way . . . Wait . . . what did you say that her name was again . . . and what did you mean by 'things' in there?"

In spite of all the chaos, Brad couldn't help but grin at Tom's opportunism there. "Her name is usually Helga Howard until she marries a Tom Tedesco. Also, I said 'things' because they could have been shape shifters from planet Z. But they have stayed out of this war, and they tend not to do well in portal travel."

Then Brad added, "We'll have an investigator here shortly to evaluate what happened, and they'll likely get to the bottom of it."

Then another portal opened not far off in the woods near where they had come back. Tom and Brad saw the flash of shimmering light from it and grabbed two laser cannons and a couple of soldiers who were nearby and rushed towards the general area of the light flash.

They arrived at the portal to see Melanie (still in courtroom appropriate dress in the middle of the arctic in spring) standing at the edge of the portal waiting for them. They had the two soldiers stand at the perimeter of the area near the portal as they ran forward to Melanie.

"You need a parka!" Tom yelled in a confused outburst.

"The Dagor came back to the swamp and destroyed my communications tower. I needed to get to you two. We think the Dagor tricked a Helga Howard widow and her kids to go to Tom's cabin to compromise him or her in some way," Melanie shouted out and then seemed to pass out as she collapsed. Tom leapt forward to catch her.

Tom thought she felt particularly heavy for such a thin young woman as he helped her up.

Then the reality of her words sunk in. The woman and the children destroyed in the cabin were not enemy combatants. They were victims in the cabin. A real human person, one who was a woman that was a soulmate-type person for him, had come to his cabin and been blown up by Dagor or Gavaa' bombs.

"Tom, we need to go back through that portal quickly and get her back to the swamp." Brad was yelling too, but at the same time, he was lining the three of them up to enter the portal together so as to avoid the appearance of chasing each other as they entered it.

Just as they were about to step into the portal, two Gavaa' appeared in the woods on the side of the portal opposite from where the soldiers who had accompanied them stood. And the Gavaa' were closer to the portal than Tom and Brad's support soldiers. The Gavaa' rushed towards them from the trees. Tom recognized one of them. "That's Major Bart!" he shouted. Tom and Brad rushed into the portal together as Major Bart leapt at them and intentionally stuck his arm towards them in a vain attempt to grab them. The portal pulled through Tom, Brad, and Melanie (in Tom's arms) and closed with a snap. They exited into the swamp, and a severed Gavaa' arm fell through at their feet, bleeding on the muddy ground.

"That guy doesn't learn!" Tom yelled. "Grab that thing and put it in your pack!" He barked his order to Brad. Brad didn't hesitate, ripped off his parka, and grabbed up the bleeding, twitching severed arm and threw it into his backpack. Then Brad held Melanie for a minute while Tom shed his parka. Tom took Melanie back and started down the trail.

"Oh please let's make headway; this petite woman must weigh 250 pounds. How is that possible?" Tom was complaining as soon as they got started down the trail.

Brad smiled and said, "She's 205 pounds to be exact. You shouldn't have trouble with that."

"I can handle 205, but she's five-five with a petite frame. How can she possibly be this heavy?" Tom was aghast at the thought.

"Still haven't figured it out, eh?" Brad smirked that funny smirk.

Tom's face went pale, "She's not human is she?"

"No, she's definitely not. Not Dagor or Gavaa' or any other humanoid biological creature either," Brad said as he smirked again.

Tom was completely bewildered at that revelation.

"She's an android Tom. She can handle the cold on a full charge. But I suspect she's used up a lot of power today, so that's why she didn't do as well when she hit the cold coming out of that portal near your cabin," Brad explained as he finally came clean with Tom.

"Ok, how many of you are androids?" Tom said with a concerned look.

Brad laughed before responding. Then he explained, "We use a few per planet as gatekeepers because, when fully charged, they can stay up for seven days and seven nights non-stop to watch over a portal crossing area. There are only two models in existence that I know of, and they are the Melanie and the Barbara. They're small. They're believable as humans for infiltration, and they're very powerful and reliable."

They reached the mansion and got in. Brad showed Tom the charging platform to lay Melanie on. It was just like a cot with a glow coming from it, hung from the wall. Tom laid her down and watched as the glow on the cot encircled her and started throbbing. Brad explained that it would take about two hours for Melanie to be fully charged. So they left her on the cot and went down the long hallway into the kitchen to find food.

Less than 15 minutes from the start of the charging process, Melanie showed up unannounced in the kitchen.

"Did a Gavaa' warrior lose a severed arm following us through the portal?" she asked.

"Yes," they replied in unison as they looked at each other.

"Well, it's crawling through the house and tearing things up!"

They both leapt up and ran from the kitchen to find it. The search wasn't hard as they only needed to follow the path of things torn, broken, or covered in blood along the way from Brad's backpack to a front window where it was trying to climb out. Brad snatched it up and put it in a black plastic garbage bag from the kitchen.

"We need to burn that thing, or it will grow into the full-sized child of Major Bart since he was the one who followed us and stuck his arm in," Tom asserted firmly. Then Tom wondered aloud, "Why did he do that knowing full well what would happen?"

"People do dumb things sometimes in the heat of battle Tom. Even someone experienced like Major Bart. It's my fault the arm was not destroyed right away; I should have done that first," Brad replied. Then he turned to Melanie as he started down the kitchen hallway to deal with the arm in the backyard and said, "You need to get back to the charging table."

"There's something I need to tell you both," Melanie made a concerned face. Then she continued, "I got a communication from Helga Tedesco of Earth 22 while I was charging. She was approached by Dagor sympathizers there who tried to plant a bomb in her shopping bag while they were talking to her."

"So it's officially a strategy now. They are going after all the Tom and Helga Tedescoes on every one of the interconnected, dimensional earths." Brad reached the end of the long hallway, breathed in deeply, and then said, "Tom, you understand you're a target now don't you?" Then he exploded in a ball of fire, blood, and guts.

Tom and Melanie were knocked over by the force of the blast but fell onto one of the luxurious couches that filled Melanie's mansion. Melanie rushed to a fire extinguisher (her auditory senses were not affected by the blast like a human's would be) and put out the fire. Brad was in pieces. Tom gathered himself as the ringing in his ears subsided and went to help Melanie clean up.

"They have a new strategy and new tricks to hide bombs," Melanie was assessing their discovery and calculating the implications, "They are making their own soldiers' severed limbs into living bombs."

"When Major Bart stuck his arm into the portal following us, he did it on purpose. He knew that there was an explosive implant in his arm, and he wanted us to have it nearby when it went off." Tom looked at Melanie with concern. "Is there a Helga Howard on this planet I was supposed to meet?"

"Yes, and she's part of our defense team." Melanie replied in a flat way that Tom finally caught.

"You're pretty expressive for an android, but you don't always inflect at the right time." Tom smiled and she smiled back.

"Help me get better at that Tom, but meanwhile, let's keep you safe."

Then Melanie called for another company of Hawks soldiers to guard them. They arrived within the hour and Tom went to get a night's sleep.

The next day, they received instructions from the central command to leave the mansion and come to the Hawks home-world. That evening, after they'd cleaned up and were getting ready to leave, Tom caught Melanie and said, "I'd like to meet the Helga of this world." Tom smiled warmly at Melanie.

At this notion, Melanie smiled bigger. "Ok," she said, "I'd like to help you with that."

"No need," came a melodic voice from behind them. Startled, they both whirled around to face a beautiful blonde about Tom's age standing in the front door. "I'm Helga, and I'd like to ask you Tom, *'Where have you been all my life?'*"

Tom burst out laughing. "I don't know," he said, "adventuring all over the planet and, lately, other planets, I guess."

Helga had been rounded up by the Hawks soldiers as well and had come to the bayou to join them on their journey. She and Tom spent the next ninety minutes discussing how other Toms and Helgas throughout the alternate dimensions had met. Helga had learned these tales while working for the defense force for the last year.

"I'd been kind of embarrassed, Tom, that we hadn't met since there are so many Toms and Helgas who have met."

"Well look, you are a beautiful and confident woman. Let's not put the pressure on each other that we have to live up to what some similar persons have accomplished elsewhere. I will admit that I feel a connection with you that feels like you're a childhood friend or like I've always known you. Let's enjoy that and see where it goes. I mean, I think we're going to be together now for a bit as we have to flee some alien forces in an interdimensional war that is about to erupt, but why let that hold us back?"

They both laughed at the thought. Then Melanie came back to move them forward.

"I know you two are having a great time, but we have to leave, you know. We are sitting ducks here." Melanie had been recharging one last time and came in full of energy and ready to go. She had the portal locator in her hand and announced that another portal was coming in less than ten minutes.

"Are you ok to leave this area on such quick notice?" Tom asked Helga.

Helga responded with a smile and her latest mantra, "My life changed about a year and a half ago when I was chased through the woods by a Dagor troop and learned how to jump through time and space in a living portal. I pack light now and I brought my bags."

They followed Melanie out the door and got ready for a new world.

Tom's thoughts were running wild through his head. He'd paused to fall behind Helga as they walked off the porch and to sort through his thoughts. "Am I misleading this girl? I've never connected with a woman in quite this way, and I've just met her. Am I high? No, I haven't taken anything. What if I hurt her and then all these people in this defense force think I'm an evil Tom Tedesco?" Then he snickered at himself and he made a mistake.

He looked at Helga in the moonlight as they walked out of the mansion and into the bayou to find the next portal. She glistened.

"Ah crap. She even sparkles." With that he stepped up his pace to match Helga's and Melanie's.

"Well," he said, "I'm looking forward to this adventure."

Helga smiled a warm and happy smile back, and they found the portal before the next wave of Gavaa' came.

The End... for now

Bots for Bots: A Robot Portal Story

Hot, black oil was spurting everywhere on her work table. Emm was trying to staunch the bloody flow with a wrench and fast reflexes. "Ouch!" she let out a sharp exclamation as some of the hot oil spurting out of her project flicked up in sprinkles onto her face. "Hold still B3!" She shouted at the little water collection bot as he wriggled to life while under repair. Emm cranked the last bolt and seal into place and set the little bot upright. It quickly oriented itself and scurried away to pursue its purpose.

Emm was good with bots. She was even better with the self-aware bots (talkies she called them) that were the dominant species on the planet now. In fact, Emm hadn't seen any other humans on the planet for years. She was lonely and missed their conversation. Oh talkies could talk, but weren't creative conversationally, they repeated very similar phrases, had a cold empty tone with no inflection and were sterile, indifferent company.

"Oh, I wish I had another person to talk to," she let out with a sigh.

"I can talk with you Emm," came a hollow emotionless response from Henry. Henry was the oldest running talkie that Emm knew. He did try to engage her from time to time. She would think it was charming if he was doing it with any intent, but she knew it was just good programming from the time before the bombs.

"Yes, the time before the bombs," her mind mulled the thought over as she carelessly spoke it out.

"You don't blame yourself do you Emm?" Henry queried her.

"That is an odd question for a talkie," Emm thought as she'd never heard a talkie discuss or question motives let alone assign blame or intent. "No Henry, I don't. All the humanoids in that last battle could have made other choices. I wish I had convinced more of them to unite. I would certainly change things if I could go back in time, but that definitely isn't happening."

She looked around at the odd assortment of bots, parts and discombobulated talkies. Looking at the room made her think of a mechanical museum (one that closed down long ago). Everything was dusty except Emm's cot and the little living area she used to keep herself feeling sane and purposeful. "What have I come to?" She wanted to break down and stop, but still she hoped. She hoped that if she kept herself sane and kept all the salvageable bots and talkies going, something would change. Some living soul with a purpose could be found, if for nothing else than companionship or commiseration.

"Remind me again Emm, how did you avoid destruction on Devastation Day?" Harvey asked.

"What is going on with you Henry? You know full well I was in the basement when the bomb dropped." She studied Henry closely knowing fully that his cold metal face wasn't going to give any non-verbal communication. She would have thought he was having a hard drive failure except that such a failure usually results in gibberish from a talkie. These questions were personal, conversationally appropriate and they weren't recycled or amalgamated, pre-programmed phrases from his hard drive. "He was using the phrase, "remind me again" to get me to open up and share my sense of fault or blame," she thought.

"I know Emm, but I've been pondering your circumstance for these last several years and while I can't understand emotions, I understand what fuels them, your experiences and your place in them."

Emm was staring at Henry in amazement at this seeming breakthrough moment for a talkie when they were abruptly interrupted by a huge explosion outside. They rushed out of the building they called home to find a fire burning in the water reclamation mill. One of the bots had slipped too close to a cog in the grand machine and gotten caught up in it. A domino falling set of events occurred and the bot and the mill sparked and a conflagration took off. Rescue bots and talkies were scurrying everywhere to either avoid the fire or get the fire under control. Emm hadn't seen such a hubbub since the last time she'd seen a person alive on the planet.

Emm barked out orders to the multitude of talkies and bots that had voice command. "Go to the shed and get back up extinguishers," she shouted to one, "you go and get any bromochlorodifluoromethane out of the lab" she shouted to another. New production of bromochlorodifluoromethane had been banned many years before due to its effect on the planet's ozone, but she knew that they had reserves of it and now was the time to use it.

Henry had scurried about to get combustible items in or around the melee out of the way. Emm continued directing the bots through hours of containment and extinguishment efforts until dawn. She was exhausted and decided to sit to take a moment to absorb the full weight of all the destruction she'd just witnessed.

"Oh, Emm what have you let happen?" Emm moaned aloud as she let out a huge sigh and dropped to the lip of a set of concrete stairs at the edge of the complex.

Henry was coming back by from his latest trip between the mess and the temporary garbage dump that they'd created for garbage bots to haul off pieces of the destruction. "I don't think you let that happen Emm," he said (with his what now seemed to be exceptionally hollow sounding voice), "you have tirelessly worked to keep this place up for years in the vain hope that others had survived besides yourself. You have only preserved or improved it."

Emm stared at Henry again for what seemed like an eternity.

"How are you doing that?" she questioned him. "You don't have biological components; you are built on the old binary systems of the past. You should not be able to formulate creative, situational, emotionally appropriate responses to a tragic event like this in context unprompted by me!"

Henry stared back at Emm. His cold metal face was nothing but plates, bolts, screws and hinges. He didn't have artificial flesh molded over his features. He couldn't express emotions via that mouth even if he had been built with an emotional capacity. Henry stared until his metal lips opened a crack and then he shattered Emm to the core. "I know who you are."

"What?" She stood up to stare at Henry, "what are you talking about? I'm Emm and you've known me since the bomb. I've lived here all my life."

"No, you came from another civilization before this one was destroyed. You were part of a team that was formed to fight the Dagor and the Gaveena. Our world wasn't as advanced as yours and our human population hoped that you and your people would save them. They thought with your advanced tech and weapons and your plans for unity that there was hope for us." Henry had turned open his conversational floodgates as he suddenly poured out his secret knowledge.

"There you go again surprising me Henry. You just said "us" when you talked about the human population. You aren't one of us. You are a robot!" Emm was thinking about running to the supply room for a weapon. Then Henry held up a tiny chip he'd carried in a little compartment on his chest.

"What is that?" Emm demanded.

"It's a human emotion, logic and adapt chip for androids. It enables the most advanced androids known in the multitude of universes to think and feel and hide among humans." Henry asserted.

"What good would that do you and how do you know that's what it is?" Emm hesitated as a memory pulled at the back of her mind.

"I know what it is because I've studied android technology for the last four years since the bomb. I was an intelligence recording talkie before the bomb. My job was to gather foreign tech and assimilate it. When the bomb hit and all the humans here died, I kept doing my job. I collected foreign tech, learned its design and assimilated it."

Emm felt a churning in her stomach, she wasn't sure what she was dealing with in Henry. This was uncharted territory for any talkie she'd dealt with. "I see Henry, you've become a robot with emotions and improved your vocabulary. Wonderful, what's next? Will you learn to fly?"

Then Emm gained a fortuitous moment. An explosion behind Henry caused him to turn. Emm kicked him in a hinged spot and he slipped on the steps and tumbled down the flight of them. Emm ran to the storage building.

"Where is that blaster!" Emm yelled as she desperately searched for a weapon of significance to terminate Henry. Seemingly in response to her outburst, a little collector bot scurried across the floor and grabbed the blast gun she'd been looking for off the shelf across from Emm. "Good boy!" Bring it here she exclaimed.

The bot started across the room towards Emm just as Henry got to the door. Then Emm gasped as the bot turned and delivered the blaster to Henry.

"Bots for bots dear. I programmed them to obey me a week ago. Surprised Emm?" Henry asked, "or should I call you 'Melanie'?"

The pit in Emm's stomach churned, "what are you talking about?" she asked, but that deep memory pulling at the back of her mind kept coming back, "What is that thought?"

"You were a violent, successful weapon for the humans that came here to protect us. Your name was Melanie and you are an android." Henry's face still held no emotion, but the voice seemed to inflect more than ever now. The inflection Melanie heard was one of contempt.

"You know it's true don't you?" Henry continued.

The pit in her stomach churned more, "No I don't know what you're talking about." Then, she felt weak and wanted to lie down, "why am I feeling so weak?" she thought.

"Don't worry Melanie; I won't destroy you even though you were going to destroy me. I need to learn more from you." With that Melanie ran out of power and fainted onto the ground.

Henry picked up Melanie's android body and carried her back to the building they kept her living space in. He pulled the blankets on her cot back and laid her carefully in the middle of it. Then he snapped restraints on. He turned on the charging system and let Melanie begin to re-charge.

"I'll need you Melanie. You've deceived yourself for four years, I don't know if you were damaged by the concussive force of the bomb or if the radioactive fallout affected your AI, but we need to get back in the fight. I blame your leaders and I'll punish them in time, but first, we have to win the war."

In another time and place, Tom Tedesco discovers a portal in space.

Lonely: A Space Portal Story

"Something isn't right," rolled in a whirling delirium about Tom's head. Spinning lights and the sounds of his supply rocket spun around him. He felt blood on his forehead and the smack of the pilot's console against his head. Snap, he was awake again as his head and torso bobbed up and down from the console to the back of his chair. He'd banged his head on the console as his seat belt harness had not been set. As he became aware of his surroundings, he caught the acrid smell of melting electrical wires coming from the now bloody console in front of him. He remembered where he was but not what had just happened.

"Hello," he shouted out. "Oh that's right," his short-term memories flooded back in, "I'm alone."

He'd run into a small, unexpected, and unmapped asteroid belt.

"What have I done?" he muttered. Tom had a bad habit of blaming himself for things that were truly outside of his control. "Where am I? What am I going to do about this?" he bellowed out as he began assessing his situation.

Tom had been sent on a scouting and mapping mission and given supplies to run between Earth and Mars. NASA had achieved several meaningful breakthroughs over the last 20 years that allowed us to set up a base on Mars, and we'd circled around Venus and Jupiter on manned missions. We were traveling much faster now, but still not at the kinds of speeds it would take for manned interstellar travel.

AI had progressed to the point that a crew was no longer needed for work purposes. Tom was supposed to run supplies from Earth to the base on Mars, and, yes, we were now trying to do supply runs with one pilot in a ship. Tom was actually the first to be sent out alone. Accountants don't calculate very well the human element and the need for conversation.

"I didn't realize how lonely this would be," he muttered while pulling up navigational controls and information. He gazed out over the dark, starlit vista from his ship's windows, "So beautiful . . . but weird . . ." Something wasn't right. He wasn't supposed to be coming up on Mars for another 36 hours, but there was a planet right in front, coming up fairly quickly. "How long was I knocked out?" was running through Tom's head while he stared at the impending planet before him.

"That doesn't even look like Mars! . . . What is happening here?" Tom struggled to get a read on where he'd been or how long he'd been knocked out. "I need to remember everything that happened." He pulled on foggy memories from the moment the asteroid wave first hit. The hair on his arms stood up as a dense, creepy memory rolled in. He'd seen something in the asteroid belt before he blacked out.

"What was it?" he muttered out loud. He remembered that inside the asteroid belt, he'd seen a shimmer and what looked like a hole in space or a pool of water. In fact, it was almost like a mirror . . . a liquid mirror. That didn't make sense.

"Man, it would be good to have someone to talk to now," was rolling around in his head, "I need to bounce around what I know and what I don't."

The communications system came on with a strange outburst of data from the planet ahead, "bzztt . . . [unintelligible words are uttered] . . ."

"What?" said Tom. He depressed a communications channel and spoke into the communication mic, "This is Tom Tedesco on Mars Freight 101."

The same message came back, "bzztt . . . [the same unintelligible phrase] . . ." A little stronger but no clearer this time . . . and Tom noticed a very strange lisp in the voice of the speaker.

"Is this a transmission from earth?" Tom queried back into the communicator.

"No earth transmission should be able to bounce off Mars and get picked up by me," he thought. "But that was a clear communication, and it certainly wasn't in English." Tom's stomach started to churn.

The planet, though still quite a ways away, was coming into view out his front shields. His body froze, and all fear indicators in his metabolism kicked in. The planet had oceans and multi-colored continents. Tom was paralyzed for more than just a moment as the realization sunk in. "That isn't Mars, Earth, or any planet in my solar system!" he croaked out.

"bzztt . . . [again with the unintelligible phrase]." The communication was getting louder and started to seem slightly irritated. It was the perfect smelling salt to Tom's system. He jumped out of his frozen state and turned to the navigation controls looking for the Re-Trace system. He wasn't sure if anyone even knew why they built something like that into the navigation systems, but he felt like it was his best chance to reverse course and possibly get back exactly the way he came.

Then the logic in that idea seeped in and made him want to melt away. Tom was now convinced that he was in a different solar system. He was also sure he'd only been out for an hour or two, and the ship's internal controls seemed to back that up. Further, if whatever brought him here in such a short time was moving with the asteroid belt, then, surely, it was a moving target. So his use of the Re-Trace system would only take him back to an area where the asteroid belt and the shimmer had been—not where it had moved to. Still, it had merit. If he could pinpoint where it had been, he might see it again sweeping through the same path in cycles. Either way, he knew he should not proceed towards the strange communication he was getting as he continued towards the planet.

So Tom kicked on the Re-Trace system. The ship swung wide while the navigation computer did calculations and aligned the ship on a path back the way it had come. Tom gulped in the stale canned air of the ship's oxygen tanks and held on as the ship started to accelerate along the reverse path. Nothing looked right, but, worse, he didn't have sufficient data points to try to calculate when the ship had left his solar system and where it entered this one. He did know there would be a loose trail of fuel vapors floating in space along the way back, and he quickly commanded the ship's onboard sensors to track the vapors and flag when they stopped.

After a tense hour of travel, the ship's onboard computer indicated that there was a diminishing trail of fuel vapor in front of it. Tom slowed the ship's forward momentum. "If that asteroid belt carries whatever that shimmer was with it, I might not see it come through here again for a year," he thought for a moment and pondered the implications of that. He didn't have those levels of supply—not even close—and he assumed he'd go crazy if he was stuck here for a year alone. Things became so quiet as he slowed down further. He could hear every creak, tick, and pop the ship made as it progressed. "Man, this is lonely, as lonely as a tick on an iceberg." Tom pitied himself now.

"I need a miracle," he thought . . . then it happened. Up ahead, he saw the shimmer. "What are you?" . . . "Forget that, you're my miracle portal" . . . "Just what I need."

He didn't have to adjust course on the Re-Trace system. The portal was right where it had been. If there had been an asteroid belt, it was on the other side of the portal, so no problems entering from this side. The converse would likely not be true. That realization sank in for Tom. If he entered this side in calm, open space, the other side would probably still have the asteroid storm going on as he exits the portal.

"Oh crapola!" Tom rushed to strap back into his captain's chair. He made sure the chest strap was on securely this time.

"Clunk." A strange noise on the back side of the supply ship occurred just before Tom got to the portal. Then he entered it. The ship was making all sorts of strange noises like it was being twisted and bounced inside of a massive clothes dryer. Boom . . . he was out.

Explosive sounds of pelting rocks blasts through the internal atmosphere of the ship. The hail storm of meteorites from the other side of the portal started pelting his ship. Like rail guns raining rock and granite bullets down on the ship in a flood. He looked up and knew relief was in sight. The portal sat at the edge of the asteroid belt in our solar system. He punched the ship through the last of the belt, relaxed, and recalibrated navigation to circumvent it as he turned the ship to head back on the original journey to provide supplies to Mars.

"I made it, and I've found a portal to a new universe!" he exclaimed. Tom knew he was safe and quietly pondered the significance to the world and to himself of his discovery.

He was well on his way to Mars too. He relaxed and sat back in his chair to take a nap as the ship proceeded calmly on its quiet journey through space.

Epilogue:

*** The following conversation is completely translated language.

****"bzztt . . . Tell me our probe was able to launch a space walker towards and latch onto the strange ship marked "NASA" that was approaching Mezzors before it reversed?" Director Gaul of Mezzors questioned with disdain.

"Yes," said General Vim, "now that we have our man attached to NASA, we can get reports back from him and see where these unknown ships come from and why they are able to get their ships through the portal when ours won't go."

"It's incredibly convenient that we had a large military ship in that area before it was able to disappear through the temporal portal. Have we certainty that our man got through?" questioned the Director.

"As you know, we've gotten small individuals in space walking suits to go through and come back. We've just never been able to get ships through . . . They won't even enter at all. Nevertheless, our thought this time was to latch a walker onto the NASA ship and to let him ride it through then report back to us."

"I know all that," said the Director. "Have you received any communications from the walker? And who is he?"

"He's lieutenant Bezor, and we haven't yet. But sir, when we've had ships that the portal rejects, they just couldn't enter at all, so we have every reason to believe he's through. We've seen nothing on this side . . . wait, there's something small near the portal entrance . . ."

The aliens paused their radio communications as the General's ship approached the portal.

"It's a severed arm from the walker . . ." the General was aghast. "Why did the portal partially let him through and leave his arm here?"

On the other side of the portal, clinging with magnetic clasps to the back of Tom's ship, was Bezor, minus an arm and wailing in his lizard tongue . . . "bzztt, bzztt, bzztt" . . .

Mirage: a Young Tom Tedesco Portal Story

"That can't be real," Tom's scattered mind was trying to comprehend what his dry, bloodshot eyes were telling him.

"It must be a mirage!"

But there it was. Shimmering in the dry desert heat. As he stumbled across the top of a sand dune, Tom saw what looked like a seven-foot-tall mirror made of water floating up from the sand. It beaconed him to come.

Tom was too dry, parched, and exhausted to argue. He'd been lost in the desert for 24 hours now, and he was in bad need of water. No roads or signs of people had been around him since his 4Runner hit a big rock in an off-the-pathway trail and ran out of oil. He'd been wandering ever since.

"Does that thing have water in it?" he muttered. No mind. He was stumbling towards it as he contemplated its meaning and purpose. Sheer exhaustion and desperation powered his body to push on towards it.

As he got within a few feet, he spotted movement right in front of it.

"What is that?!" His pink, dry, tired eyes popped out like balloons on a helium tank. There was a severed leg lying in front of the shimmer. It was fresh with blood and was still twitching and moving. Now he wanted to run, but he had no strength to do it.

"Oh crap! What did that, and who was it?" Now he was terrified.

His logical mind wanted to consider how to examine the shimmer. His primal parts said to run. Then water, a tiny splash, came from the shimmer and hit the dry sand at its base. Away, away it evaporated from the dry arid sands. The appearance of water, even those few drops, changed everything.

"Should I throw something at this shimmer or find a stick to push into it?" he tried to argue with himself, but the desperate, emotional, primal part of his brain said, "I'm in charge, and we're going in." He leaped into the shimmer.

Splash!

"Water!" he shrieked out like a little school girl.

He was standing just inside the edge of a crystal clear, evergreen lined lake. Specifically, he was in a bay on the lake where a beautiful and cold mountain stream was flowing into it. He threw himself deeper into it and gulped and gulped, swallowing and drinking it all in. "Ecstasy! I'm saved!" he was squealing out loud and laughing at himself for it. Nothing refreshes like a cool mountain stream pouring into a bay. "Ah, water, peace, and relaxation . . ."

His immediate need for fresh water sated, he waded back to the edge of the lake and looked back at the shimmer.

Immediately, the hairs on the back of his neck stood up! There was a mountain lion (or something that looked like one) with an oddly shaped head blocking his path back to the shimmer. He froze and surveyed the scene. The big cat was looking right at him, and its tail was swishing. Its head was elongated and triangular. Its paws were almost . . . like hands . . . or something in between hands and paws???

"It's a paw but with an opposable thumb-like digit!" Tom's mind was screaming to him now!

"Where am I? What have I gotten myself into? This isn't Africa, and that's not like any big cat I've ever seen on Wild Safari shows."

He knelt and picked up a large rock out of sheer instinct. Then he paused. He wanted to run or throw the rock . . . or both!

"Maybe I can confuse it if I charge it and then dive into the shimmer," his mind was racing with options.

But the brain is a mysterious thing. While his brain was racing with options, it was evaluating the behavior of the big cat. The cat wasn't attacking. It wasn't curling its lips to show teeth. It wasn't growling or getting down on haunches to pounce. Instead, it was acting like it wanted his attention and wanted a signal to approach.

The cat bent down slightly and picked up an object. Tom squinted but couldn't quite see what it was. Then the cat moved a few steps towards him.

Tom reacted by going into a runner's crouch.

The cat paused and then approached with his side towards Tom. Tom's brain new it was not an aggressive approach even if his nerves didn't. He still wanted to throw the rock and run towards the shimmer. But, he held. As the cat closed the distance once more, it stopped and reached out its paw with the object it had picked up.

Tom's hand trembled, but he reached out with his free hand and took the object. It was a key of some type. The cat sat on its hind legs and started purring a loud, weird, whistling-like purr. It pawed at Tom like a dog trying to shake hands. Tom reached out and shook the cat's paw. At first, it shook his hand. Then the cat pulled on his hand for a second and turned towards a road that led down to the lake. The cat wanted him to look up in order to see the road

That was when Tom saw it . . . the blood. There was a blood trail from the side and edge of the shimmer up towards the road like one would see left behind by a person with a severed leg. Then it tapered off like someone had helped to tie up the wound. There were drag marks like the injured person was pulled to a point, and then there were strange track marks on the road. An unusual vehicle had pulled away with the injured person plus others. The cat was getting excited now. He was purring louder and pacing and looking up the road. He wanted Tom to follow. Tom was torn. The shimmer was the way back to . . . home and potential safety if he could get through the desert, but the road . . . it held the excitement of possibility and *danger*.

Tom started to follow the cat up the road when a voice called out, "Hey there!" and, "Who are you?"

Startled and shook, Tom froze and looked up. There was a beautiful girl in what looked like old west or Indian style leather clothes and boot moccasins. She was a dish water blonde with a great figure and striking blue eyes.

"I see you've met Leo," she offered.

"Hi," was about all Tom could get out for a few seconds. Then he came out of his stupor, "I'm Tom. I was wandering in the Arizona desert for a day when I found that!" He pointed back to the shimmer.

"It brought me here to water, and I was desperately in need of it," he said.

"Yes, that's how my great grandfather found this place over 100 years ago," the girl stated.

Tom suddenly became aware of what a disheveled ragamuffin he looked like. He'd been wandering in the desert for a day, jumped in a lake for water, and was now air drying his previously soaked clothes in the light breeze of wherever this was.

"I must look a mess . . . what did you say your name was?" he brokenly blurted out.

"I didn't, but I'm Helga," she said.

"I saw the bloody trail and thought I should follow it. Or, Leo did," Tom started to explain.

"Oh, yes, that was from our sheriff. He got careless coming back in the portal. You can't chase others or they shut off mid-transport. We learned that a long time ago. My father thinks it's a defense mechanism for the portal. They seem to be a living thing or an appendage of one, and they always protect prey from predators."

That was a lot for Tom. He'd found a "magic" portal, and now here was a girl on the other side telling him it's a natural phenomenon. And her family has been using it and studying it for years?

"How many of you are there here? And, where is here?" he asked.

"About a hundred of us, mostly the original settler's direct descendants, but with the exception of me, they all stopped at generation two. So I'm the youngest one here." She smiled innocently at her situation.

"Helga, your giant cat with hand paws gave me this key thing," Tom extended it out to Helga.

She giggled at his description of Leo. "Oh thanks! I did need that for the sheriff's house. In between screaming about his leg, he was asking for us to get something out of his house that would help him hold the portal open so we could get his leg back and maybe reattach it . . . But I think that's a long shot even with our portal technology."

"Helga, I saw his leg right before I entered the portal. Do you need me to go back and get it? . . . wait . . . What about your technology?"

"If you do go back, you can probably push the leg through, but you can't come back right away. You know that, right?" she asked as though he should know it.

"No, I didn't know that, but if it will spare a man his leg, I'll go back through." Tom was starting to feel a little heroic now, "But what about your technology?"

"You'll need supplies and water," Helga started assessing the opportunity, "It would be good to try, and we do have to hurry." Helga jumped on an pristine, classic CR 125 dirt bike she'd hidden in the woods and said, "Wait here with Leo. I'll be right back."

She burst away like a house afire. Leo rolled around contentedly on his back. Tom paced around considering everything that he'd just learned.

Crazy thoughts were bugging him, "These people knew and understood the portals. They've been here for generations, and they have special technology?" he questioned himself, ". . . and why did I feel so comfortable with that girl like I've met her somewhere before? And where did she get that awesome CR 125?"

Less than five minutes passed, and she was back with a canteen full of water and cheese and bread in a sack along with a compass. She blazed up, threw the bike down, and gave Tom the supplies.

"If you go through the portal, you'll be back in the desert where you were. Carefully push the leg through and don't let your hands follow it too far. After you push the leg through, go Northwest from the portal's exit for half a day, and you'll reach a small town with a convenience store. You'll be okay."

Tom had already walked back to the portal and was ready to re-enter it. He looked at her and laughed at himself as he blurted out, "Can I come back and see you again?"

She looked at him with amazement and searched his eyes for a purpose. She blushed a little.

"Yes, but you'll need to watch the weather and the moon for the signs to tell you when the shimmer is going to reappear. This one comes the day after the first full moon following a rain. Since it doesn't rain much in the Arizona desert, it won't come back again for about 6 months"

He stared at her, wondering how they'd come to understand so much about it.

Then she shoved him towards the shimmer and said, "You have to hurry or that leg will be too far damaged to reattach." But, as she pushed on him, she came close. He met her eyes, and then she kissed him lightly and pleaded, "Go . . . hurry."

He pushed through the shimmer, and there he was back in the desert. He was startled by avian screams as buzzards had landed and were just starting to peck at the leg. They released it upon his appearance, but they didn't immediately fly away. Tom picked up a large rock and threw it at them, and they squawked and yielded a few feet. He rushed in and grabbed the leg. They flew off squawking and fussing and giving him what seemed like dirty looks for buzzards. He picked up the leg and walked towards the portal. Carefully, he shoved the leg through the portal and released it just as it was going in. He couldn't see Helga or the leg once he released it, but he felt like he had gotten it successfully pushed through. Then the shimmer wavered. It vibrated and made a small squelching sound then evaporated. He pulled the compass Helga had given out of his pocket and started heading northwest. At least now he had water and food and knew a general direction to head.

"I never thought I'd be a weather man or a lunar maniac, but I guess I'll be both now," he chuckled to himself. He had a reason to watch the signs. He desperately wanted to know more about Helga, her people, and the "portal technology" she claimed they had.

As he plodded off, he felt a tinge of hair along his spine move up. He looked back, but he couldn't see anything.

Off in the distance, something was watching him. He felt it, but he didn't want to give it away, so he turned back northwest and kept moving. "I'm coming back Helga," he said aloud. Inside his head churned phrases of concern for Helga, "Leo you better earn your dinner protecting that girl . . ." but his body knew things weren't well. His stomach churned as he pushed his way back to civilization.